Justice and Joy

A White Mountains Romantic Mystery

Jane Firebaugh

This book is a work of fiction. Names, characters, places, and incidents are products of the author's imagination or are used fictitiously. Any resemblance to actual events or locales, or any person, living or dead, is entirely coincidental.

Cover designed by Jane Firebaugh

ISBN-13: 978-1543067972

ISBN-10: 1543067972

DEDICATION

To all who truly love.

ACKNOWLEDGEMENTS

I would like to thank my awesome Beta Readers and Proof Readers for their generous donation of time and energy, and all my friends (offline and online) who encouraged me.
And to all my readers, thank you so much for supporting my books!
You all rock!

Table of Contents

How do I love thee? Let me count the ways.
I love thee to the depth and breadth and height
My soul can reach, when feeling out of sight
For the ends of Being and ideal Grace.
I love thee to the level of every day's
Most quiet need, by sun and candle-light.
I love thee freely, as men strive for right;
I love thee purely, as they turn from praise,
I love thee with the passion put to use
In my old griefs, and with my childhood's faith.
I love thee with a love I seemed to lose
With my lost saints - I love thee with the breath,
Smiles, tears, of all my life! - and, if God choose,
I shall but love thee better after death.

Elizabeth Barrett Browning

CHAPTER ONE

Olivia McKenna swiveled in her seat for a second to see what was going on in the rear of the SUV. She could see her legal wards, five-year-old Emma and sixteen-month-old Sophia in the back seat. Sophia was in her rear facing car seat, playing with a set of plastic keys and Emma was sitting in her front facing one, leaning over to try to pet Molly, Olivia's Golden Retriever, secure in her crate in the back behind the children.

"I'm stuck, Aunt Livvie," Emma complained, tears starting to form in her brown eyes as she battled with her long daisy chain necklace that was firmly wedged under the armrest beside her car seat. "Make it let go."

"Hang on just a second sweetie," Olivia quickly pulled the car over and parked, jumping out to rescue the frustrated little girl.

"I just wanted to pet Molly and Sheyna," she sniffled softly, "I wish they could ride up here with us."

"I know, Pumpkin, that would be fun for everyone, but it is so much safer for them to be back there in their crates and you to be sitting properly in your seat in case we have to stop suddenly." Olivia gave Emma a kiss on the forehead, and wiped the tears from her face.

"Hi snookums," she leaned over and kissed Sophia too. "Okay kids, and Molly and Sheyna, we'll be home soon and Uncle Josh is coming over later for dinner and I know he'll be wanting to play with the four best girls ever." Olivia made sure the kids' buckles were secure and hopped back into the driver's seat.

"You mean Molly, Sheyna, Sophia and me? Are we really the best girls ever?" Emma asked wide eyed.

"You'd better believe it," Olivia assured her. "The two best two legged girls and the two best four legged girls."

"Can Sheyna sleep with me tonight?" Emma asked. "Molly slept with me last night, but Sheyna wouldn't come."

"Kitties are silly like that sometimes." Olivia smiled, "I'll see if I can talk her into being more sociable tonight, okay?"

"Okay, thank you Aunt Livvie."

"You're welcome, Honey."

Olivia drove the SUV into her driveway and rolled to a stop.

There was still some snow in the yard even though the weather had been pretty warm for March in New Hampshire's White Mountains.

She knew the weather could change any day and dump a few feet of snow right back in their laps, so she wasn't counting on putting away the shovels any time soon.

Olivia unbuckled Emma from her car seat and helped her out of the SUV, then went around and unbuckled Sophia, picking her up and grabbing a grocery bag from the floor below her.

"Come on Emmy, let's get Sophia into her playpen so we can bring Molly and Sheyna in too."

Emma followed obediently and sat down next to Sophia's playpen.

Olivia set Sophia inside with her toys and dropped the grocery bag on the kitchen counter before she hurried out to get the furry girls out of their crates.

Sheyna, a pretty long haired calico cat that Olivia had adopted a few months ago, meowed her approval at being freed from the crate and hopped down, running straight into the house.

Molly, a beautiful, reddish golden colored Golden Retriever, licked Olivia's hand before jumping down to join Sheyna in the house.

Olivia grabbed one last grocery bag and her purse and locked the SUV.

Even though the weather was relatively warm for the time of year, it was on the nippy side in the house after being gone all day, so Olivia opened the flue and added some wood to the fireplace, to get the fire burning hotter, then quickly put away the groceries.

She found Emma leaning over the top of the playpen playing with Sophia, her long wavy light brown hair dangling down to cover her face.

"You're such a good big sister, Emma," Olivia hugged her. "Here, let me lift Sophie out and let her ride her scooter so you guys can play without you having to be upside down."

Emma giggled, "I like being upside down. Do you think Uncle Josh will pick me up and put me upside down in the air when he comes over? That's almost as much fun as when he lets me fly. Maybe he'll let me be an airplane too."

"You know, I think you might be able to talk him into that," Olivia nodded. "It's pretty easy to talk Uncle Josh into playing when you've been such a good girl all day."

Emma smiled broadly, displaying one missing front tooth. "I was *so* good," she said proudly. "Sophia was good too. Maybe Uncle Josh will let her be an airplane too."

"I think he just might, Emmy," Olivia chuckled. He should be here in a couple of hours, so why don't you and Sophia play while I cut up some veggies for dinner?"

"Okay, can I use the crayons from the big box?"

"You sure can, just as long as you promise not to let Sophia eat them," Olivia took the crayons down from the high shelf. "For some reason, she seems to think they taste good, but you're such a big girl, that you know better, right?"

"Crayons aren't for eating. Veggies and candy are for eating, and bread too." Emma laughed. "Sophia is silly sometimes, isn't she?"

"Babies can be a little bit silly, like kitties, because they don't know enough about how things work, but she'll figure it out when she's bigger." Olivia smiled at the little girl, "She's a smart cookie, like her big sister."

"Cookie," Sophia said clearly. "Mama, cookie."

"Okay, Sophia, you can both have a cookie, but only one, because it will be dinner time soon." Olivia handed each of them a homemade oatmeal cookie.

She quickly chopped some veggies to have ready so she could make a vegetarian lasagna for dinner. It was a recipe her friend, Aracellys had given her, and the whole family loved it. Molly came and sat beneath her as she chopped, looking up hopefully in case something fell from the counter.

Olivia laughed, dropping a carrot into Molly's waiting mouth, "I guess a carrot or two wouldn't hurt, would it Molly? I'm going to take you and Sheyna for a nice walk as soon as Josh gets here, don't worry." She dropped another carrot, which Molly caught easily.

Once she'd finished prepping the meal and popped it in the pre-heated oven, Olivia and Molly joined Sheyna, Emma and Sophia on the floor in the living room.

"Emma, that drawing is interesting. Is that your family?"

"Yes. It's you and Uncle Josh and Sophia and Molly and Sheyna and me in the new house, see?" Emma pointed to the stick figures inside the big square that was in the center of a couple of other squares. "My family."

"It's wonderful, Sweetie." Olivia hugged her, as she felt her heart twist.

If we find her real family someday, how will any of us survive letting her go? She's already such an important part of our family. Don't think about it, Livvie; focus on the now.

"Molly pay," Sophia stated, giggling, not having yet mastered her Ls.

Olivia and Emma giggled too as they watched Molly play, rolling on her back, with her legs kicking in the air, trying to scratch her back by scooching along the floor.

She scooted around for a few more seconds, and rose to shake all over, drawing more delighted giggles from the two little girls.

"Well, Molly, did that get all your itches?" Olivia scratched Molly's back for her, chuckling.

Olivia's cell phone rang, and she hopped up to grab it.

"Hi Abby," she answered, reading the phone display.

It was her best friend, Abby McElhatten. She'd been hired to supervise the restoration of Candlewick, the old mansion they'd bought and were renovating

"Abby, I can tell from the pictures you sent that you've done a fabulous job overseeing the restoration," Olivia said warmly. "We really appreciate you agreeing to continue with it once we returned from our Christmas holiday trip. I honestly don't think we could have managed it without you, especially now that we have moved the wedding up, and we have Emma and Sophia to care for."

"I'm enjoying it a lot, not to mention you're paying me quite well," Abby laughed. *"Are you planning to get over to see it again soon? It's finally done, except for a couple of things I need your input on."*

"I'll talk to Josh as soon as he gets here. I think we can come out tomorrow, if we don't have anything pressing in the office."

"How is the new detective agency going?" Abby asked. *"I love the name, by the way, Mountain Valley Investigations . . . simple, and perfect for Birchwood."*

"Thanks, we had a hard time deciding. We wanted something quirky and fun, but professional won out in the long run." Olivia chuckled. "Cat and Mouse Investigations just didn't sound quite professional enough."

"I'm so excited about your wedding, Livvie," Abby squealed, *"I've never been a Maid of Honor before."*

"I'm excited too. I've never actually gotten married before, even though I came really close with Danny," Her voice was sad for a moment. "Emma and Sophia will be adorable Flower Girls, and you will be such a beautiful Maid of Honor."

"Is Jimmy Hill still going to be the Ring Bearer? He's pretty adorable too."

"Yes, he is, and Vicki, Pam and Julie will be the Bridesmaids. Vicki's husband, Andrew will be Josh's Best Man. My parents are flying in, so my Mam and Da will be able to walk me down the aisle." Olivia's eyes shone with happiness. "Peter, Josh's dad, will escort him down the aisle."

"Did you get the results of your adoption home study back yet?"

"Yes, and we were approved to adopt Sophia, so she will be officially ours in about six months if everything goes the way it should. Thanks for your references by the way, and for helping when we took the social worker on the tour around Candlewick."

"What are best friends for?" Abby laughed. *"Speaking of adoption, have you guys found out anything about Emma's biological family yet? How are you ever going to give her up if you do?"* Her voice sounded worried. *"She's so lucky you rescued her from those kidnappers, but I know you all must be really close by now. It's crazy that no one can find out where she came from."*

Olivia sighed, "I know, and it's going to be so hard if we ever do. I can't really talk about it right now, because little pitchers have big ears, as Mam used to say. We haven't learned anything, yet, though."

"Okay, well, I guess sometimes no news is good news." Abby said hopefully. "Listen, I've got to run. They're going to be delivering that gorgeous antique wardrobe you found for Emma's room to match her canopy bed, at any minute."

"Yay! I can't wait to see her face when she sees them." Olivia glanced at her ward with a twinkle in her eye. "Hopefully we'll see you tomorrow."

After she'd ended the call, Olivia changed Sophia's diaper and set her in her high chair in the kitchen.

"Emma, do you want to help me set the table?" she asked the five-year-old. "Remember, you have to be careful with the plates."

"I want to help you." Emma's face lit up. "I'm a good helper, aren't I, Aunt Livvie?"

"You're an excellent helper, Emma. Here, I'll hand you each plate, one by one, so it won't be too heavy."

Emma set the table with no other help from Olivia.

The oven timer buzzed, and Olivia took the lasagna out and set it on the stovetop to cool.

Molly and Sheyna raced to the front door, followed closely by Emma, as there was a knock.

"Good timing," Olivia picked up Sophia and hurried to open the door to let Josh inside. "Emma just finished setting the table, and the lasagna is ready. I'm going to take Molly and Sheyna for a quick walk, then we can eat."

Josh hugged and kissed Olivia and Sophia, then stooped to scoop Emma up and whirl her around. As soon as he set her down, he petted Molly and Sheyna.

"You're getting to be a really good kitchen helper, Emma. Did you set the table all by yourself?" Josh asked.

"Aunt Livvie handed me the plates, but I did everything else all by myself." She said proudly.

"What a big, smart girl you are getting to be." Josh ruffled her hair. Let me fix Molly's and Sheyna's food, then when they get back from their walk, we can feed them and help Aunt Livvie get the food on the table and we can all eat."

~~~

"How did it go with the possible client?" Olivia asked Josh, once the dinner was over and the children were in bed.

"It was a no-go. He was looking for someone to entrap his wife in a compromising position, so he could claim adultery in the divorce and not have to pay any alimony or child support." Josh's lip curled in disgust. "I told him what he wanted to do was illegal and that he was definitely looking at the wrong agency."

"Oh boy, I wonder if he realized he was talking to an ex-cop with lots of friends still on the job." Olivia rolled her eyes, "That wasn't a smart maneuver if he did."

"It isn't like we don't advertise the ex-cop part, so, yeah, he wasn't the best or the brightest bulb in the chandelier." Josh grinned. "I did get another call just before I left the office though, that might prove to be a legitimate case for us. We have a meeting with her tomorrow, if Annie can watch all the girls."

"I'll give her a call in a few minutes. If she's available, I'm sure she'll want Molly and Sheyna to come too." Olivia smiled. "I think she adores them even more than the human girls."

"Well, she *has* known them longer," Josh grinned. "So, the woman who called said she'd been swindled by a scam artist and she wanted us to catch him."

"Why didn't she just go to the police?" Olivia asked, puzzled. "I mean, she'll have to pay us to catch him, but the police would look for him for free."

"I got the feeling she's too embarrassed, and doesn't want it to become public knowledge that she was so gullible." Josh sobered, "You know how the newspaper publishes all of the police reports. I think she's hoping we can get the guy and make him give the money back without anyone knowing about it."

"Hmm, I'm not sure how we could do that, or even if it would be ethical, since if he doesn't get arrested for it, he can just go and do the same thing to someone else." Olivia pondered. "If we catch the guy and he gives her the money, we can't go to the police, because they wouldn't be able to prosecute him without her pressing charges, right?"

"No, they would need her to cooperate, but we could tell them about him and they could at least watch him." Josh sighed. "It's not the ideal situation, but maybe we can convince her to press charges after all. Let's just talk to her and see exactly what it is. Maybe she isn't worried about people knowing at all. I could have read it wrong."

Olivia turned the dishwasher on and straightened. "I'll go call Annie and see if she's available. Oh, Josh, are you up for going to Candlewick tomorrow? Abby called and wants us to drop by as soon as possible so she can get our input on something."

"Sure, what do you think about going after the meeting? You know, I had a thought I wanted to run by you. How would you feel about building a little office on the Candlewick property?"

"I had thought of having the office in the house, but didn't really want to have random people we don't know coming into our home." Olivia frowned in thought, "I'm just not sure how I feel about having people come to

Candlewick. How about the guy you met today. Would you want him there?"

"No, I wouldn't," Josh grimaced ruefully. "I think maybe we should look into buying one of the older homes that are for sale, along the main road, and converting it to an office building. Then, we can have a separate section for the kids, and have Annie or someone there to help with them while we're working. How does that sound?"

"That's a great idea. I want to be able to be in the office more, but I don't us want to miss out on spending time with Sophia and Emma either. I think they both need us a lot right now after all they've been through . . . especially Emma. Sophia's too young to remember much, and even though the adoption the kidnappers did wasn't legal, at least she wasn't out and out kidnapped from her parents like Emma probably was." Olivia smiled. "The converted house sounds awesome. What a perfect solution. It will be our daytime home as well as our office on the days we have office work to do."

"I agree, we can start looking right away. What time is Julie getting home?" Josh asked about her roommate, who was a Police Officer with the Birchwood PD. "Is she on the late shift right now?"

"No, that starts next week, I think. She had a date, actually," Olivia grinned. "I'm taking it as a good sign that she isn't back yet. If it was awful, she'd have been home by now."

"I hope he's a good guy and not one of the weirdos that just want to know how many people she's shot, or one who thinks she'll want to handcuff him."

"Ugh," Olivia rolled her eyes, "I hope not too. She is such a great person. She really doesn't need to be subjected to dates like that."

"Yeah, those are not fun. I had a few myself when I was on the job before we met. They were awkward to say the least."

Molly jumped up from beneath their feet and trotted to the front door, as Julie, Olivia's roommate, walked in.

"Hi guys," she smiled, bending to pet Molly on her way into the living room. "What are you up to tonight?"

"Not much, we've been discussing what to do about office space." Olivia grinned. "How did your date go?"

"Actually, it wasn't bad, but I think Greg and I were meant to be just friends, not anything else. We have a lot in common, but no sparks at all, just a fun time, laughing over dinner."

"Well, friends are just as good and sometimes better," Olivia agreed. "You can never have too many friends."

"I'm not in a rush to find a boyfriend or anything, so it worked for me." Julie smiled. "At least it was a fun night and I think we'll hang out together sometimes. How are the kids?" she changed the subject.

"They're sleeping now. They did great at dinner and Sophia is doing a tiny bit better every night at feeding herself." Josh chuckled. "At least there's as much food going into her mouth as onto her clothes now."

"Go, Sophia." Julie cheered. "She and Emma are both such cuties. I'm going to miss them, as well as Molly and Sheyna, when you guys move into Candlewick. Of course I'll miss you too," she added, laughing.

"I know we will miss you as well, Julie, but we'll all be visiting each other plenty often, I'm sure." Olivia hugged her friend. "Are you still planning to adopt a dog or cat once we're moved out?"

"Yes, definitely, it will be way too quiet here otherwise. Besides, I've been wishing I could have a pet for ages, so I'm really excited about it."

"I hate to leave so soon after you got home, Julie, but I also know how early you have to get up, if you're still on the day shift." Josh said knowingly. "We have a fairly early meeting too."

"Oh my stars, I forgot to call Annie." Olivia jumped up and hurried to make the call before it was too late to be civil.

"Whew," she laughed, coming back into the room. "Annie was delighted to babysit and said to make sure Molly and Sheyna came too."

"Good, and now that everything is set, I'm off to my apartment." Josh gathered Olivia in his arms for a sweet goodnight kiss.

"On that mushy note, I am off to bed," Julie laughed. "Goodnight you guys."

"Goodnight Julie," Josh and Olivia chuckled.

CHAPTER TWO

Annie and the girls were all happy to see each other, so Olivia was able to leave without feeling any guilt.

She remembered to take stock of any homes she saw for sale along the route from Annie's house to the little rented office she and Josh were using. There was one really cute two story house that looked like it would be fairly easy to convert into half home/daycare and half office. Olivia stopped and wrote down the address and the phone number for the realtor so Josh could take a look and they could call about it if he liked it too.

She arrived at the office in time to share a second cup of coffee with Josh before their prospective client was due to appear.

"I saw a nice house for conversion on the way over," she informed Josh, "It looks like it would be easy to make into exactly what we need."

"I'll give the realtor a call after our meeting," Josh smiled, as she handed him the paper with the information on the house. "Maybe we can meet the realtor later this afternoon after we go to Candlewick."

"That would be perfect," Olivia agreed. "It'll be easier to tour it the first time if it's just the two of us. I don't want to have to explain it all to Emma, then disappoint her if it doesn't work out. I know she'd love it if she could come to work with us until she starts kindergarten."

"It's too bad she couldn't start already, since we think she's probably five years old." Josh shrugged, "Oh well, without any birth records, it's not easy to be sure, so I guess she'll start next year, since she missed the first few months anyway."

"Yes, it might be better this way. It's a bit hard coming into a new school setting mid-year, even in kindergarten. Maybe by the start of the new school year, we'll have figured out who she really is and where she came from." Olivia swallowed the lump that developed in her throat at the thought.

Josh put his arm around her, seeing her distress. "Yeah, I feel the same way. As much as I want to know her background, for her sake, it's gonna be freakishly hard to give her up if we do find she has parents looking for her."

A knock at the door interrupted their troubling thoughts as their client arrived for the nine o'clock meeting.

"Good morning, Mrs. Williams." Josh opened the door and led her in, motioning to a seat. "I'm Josh Abrams. We spoke on the phone yesterday. This is Olivia McKenna, my business partner and fiancé."

"Good morning," the portly middle aged woman greeted them. "Please call me Elaine." She dropped gratefully into the proffered chair.

"Alright, Elaine, you told me that you'd been swindled, but you didn't give me much information on the case yet, so what exactly occurred?" Josh asked, as he and Olivia seated themselves at the round table with the woman.

"I feel a little foolish over the whole thing," she replied with a grimace. "I should be old enough not to fall for a scam, but I guess old doesn't necessarily mean wise."

"You're certainly not old, and obviously you're wise enough to not want to let the scammer get away with it, so I'd have to say you're being too hard on yourself." Olivia remarked kindly.

"Thanks for that," Elaine smiled, "I really have no excuse for being conned. It just sounded like a dream come true, and I wanted it to be real so badly I didn't stop to listen to my gut, which would have told me it was too good to be true."

"It's easy to do that," Olivia commiserated. "We all have things we dream of and a really smooth con artist can talk their way past our reasoning at times."

"Yes, he sure did that," she sighed. "Ever since I was a teenager, I dreamed of having a little cottage on a lake where I could afford to spend the summers and bring my grandchildren to visit."

She shook her head in disgust, "Well, this man I met in town, Roger Manning, heard me talking to a friend about that dream and offered to sell me a cottage on Little Squam Lake. He said it was being sold by someone who was desperate for a quick sale and was willing to take a huge loss on the property. The amount he was asking was much less than a cottage on that lake should cost, so at first I was suspicious, but Roger agreed to meet with me later and take me to see the cottage."

"So he actually had keys to the place and took you there?" Josh's eyebrows rose.

"Yes, I still don't know how he got the keys, but he opened the door and showed me around and everything. I fell in love with the place immediately. It was everything I'd always wanted."

"So you agreed to purchase it?" Olivia asked. "How did he propose doing the sale?"

"He had papers all drawn up with a deed that was signed by the supposed owner and everything. I just had to give him a cash payment."

She paused, looking miserable, "I know it was stupid, but it seemed so legitimate, that I went right to the bank and withdrew the money. He gave me the deed, which he said I needed to file with the county, and the keys to the cottage." She sighed heavily, "It wasn't until I went to file the deed that I realized it was all a scam and that he had no right to sell the property at all. I just had a worthless piece of paper and keys to someone else's cottage to show for it."

"That's horrible." Olivia said sadly. "I can see how you could have been taken in. How much money did he get?"

"Fifty thousand dollars," Elaine replied shakily, "A lot more than I could afford to throw away. I really thought I would have something that would be a great investment as well as a wonderful place to bring the grandkids during the summer. So I've basically trashed my life's savings and will never have anything like I'd dreamed of."

Well, you came to us to hopefully keep that from being the case," Josh consoled her. "We will do our best to find him and get your money returned." He paused, "Why *did* you come to us instead of going to the police? Were you worried about people finding out about it?"

She chuckled wryly, "Only my daughter. She's a Sergeant on the Birchwood PD. If you find him, I know she'll have to know about it then, but at least he'll be found, and hopefully I'll have the money back before she hears about it. Otherwise, I'll feel like a total fool if she and her co-workers know I've lost all that money. She'd be so embarrassed."

"Oh, your daughter must be Lily Meeks." Josh smiled. "I can see your dilemma. She'd probably be the one in charge of the case if you reported it to the local PD."

"Exactly."

"So, you won't have a problem, pressing charges against the guy if we locate him, then?" Olivia asked. "We were a little worried about that, since if he wasn't prosecuted, he'd probably just keep conning other people."

"Oh, I won't have any problems pressing charges against the smooth talking creep," her voice had a bite. "As long as I get my money back, I won't even be too embarrassed. I just don't want my daughter and the cops she works with to think I can't manage my own affairs without her help. I hate looking like an idiot."

"I can't imagine your daughter thinking you were an idiot, but I can understand how you feel. We'll do our best to get your money back as well as catching this guy before he does the same to someone else," Josh stated firmly. "I actually feel good about putting con artists in jail. I don't have a high tolerance for people that prey on other people's dreams like that. Our dreams are what give us hope."

"Thank you both. I really was hoping you'd take the case. I know you used to be a State Trooper, Josh . . . and Olivia, I read in the papers about you helping to solve a couple of local murders, so I have every confidence in your abilities to catch this man." Elaine took out her checkbook. "How much of a retainer would you need to start?"

Josh glanced at Olivia, who gave him an almost invisible shake of her head.

"We would be happy to start your case without a retainer. Normally our fees are as I told you on the telephone, but your case is one we both would like to work on pro bono." Josh rushed on, anticipating her refusal, "It will be a service to the whole community to get this guy off the streets."

"I don't want to be a pity case," Elaine started, "I may have lost most of my savings, but I'm not asking for charity."

"Please don't feel like we are offering charity," Olivia answered. "We would do this for free for anyone in the community who'd lost their savings to a con artist like that. Josh is right; it is our way of performing a community service. You're obviously a strong woman, and you'll survive even if you don't get your money back. But, if he isn't stopped, the next person he cons may be someone who would be destroyed by it."

Elaine thought for a moment in silence. "You're good people. I'll take you up on it then. This is everything I have from him, if you don't mind making me photocopies. I will leave the originals with you in case his fingerprints are still on them somehow."

"That's great. I'll make copies right now," Josh took the folder and using gloves, quickly photocopied all the documents inside. I'm going to take your prints too, so I'll know which ones to rule out if I find any."

Elaine looked slightly flustered as he proceeded to fingerprint her.

"I feel like a criminal." She chuckled. "At least you didn't have to take a mug shot."

"We'll keep you posted on anything we discover." Olivia smiled as she handed her one of their cards, after giving her a damp cloth to clean the ink off her fingers. "Please don't hesitate to call us if you think of anything else that might be helpful or if you happen to see him or hear from him again."

"I'll be sure to do that," Elaine hoisted herself to her feet and took the photocopies from Josh. "I doubt he'd have the nerve to contact me, but I guess you never know. He definitely has plenty of nerve to be able to pull that off. What would he have done if the real owners happened to show up while he was taking me through the cottage?"

"Yes. You're right. It would have been a rather risky thing to do, but he probably had researched the place and the owners, and knew their usual schedule for visiting the property, so it was likely to be safer than it looks," Josh inserted. "Most con artists are pretty meticulous about their research."

"Well, I am learning a lot from this, if nothing else," Elaine made a weak attempt at humor. "I'll be crossing my fingers and hoping to hear good news from you soon."

"So," Josh took his fingerprinting tools and started working on the documents, "I'm wondering if Elaine is the first local victim. I'm sure that if he isn't caught, she won't be the last."

"I'll ask Julie tonight if there have been any reports filed with the Birchwood PD that might be related," Olivia stated.

"Good idea," Josh agreed. "I'll give Bob O'Brian a call later to see if the State Police has heard anything about a con artist operating in the valley."

"I wish we had a way of knowing if there were other victims who haven't gone to the police because they were ashamed." Olivia sighed. "I'm afraid some people may have been too worried about looking foolish."

"Unfortunately, that *is* quite likely to happen, which is another reason we need to get this guy quickly." Josh thumped his chair down as he stood. "Con artists may not be murderers, at least not as a rule, but they can destroy people's lives nonetheless."

"It really is a pretty despicable crime, isn't it?" Olivia shook her head sadly. "Poor Elaine, he made her think she could finally have something she'd always wanted, then snatched away her hopes along with her money."

"I got a couple of decent partial prints off the contract, so we might have a lead to start out with." Josh said with a tinge of excitement in his voice.

"Do you want me to call Julie and see if she can get someone to run the prints for us? It's a lot closer than taking them to O'Brian would be." Olivia grinned. "Julie won't mind doing it or asking someone else, if she isn't in the middle of something urgent."

"That would be the best solution, if she can get someone there to do it. It's on our way to Candlewick."

"Okay, I'll ask her about reports of scamming while I'm at it then," Olivia picked up the phone.

Josh packed up his fingerprinting gear, took pictures of the fingerprints he'd found and created a working folder for their new case while Olivia talked to Julie.

"Well, Julie says they haven't had anyone report being scammed yet, and she said that her co-worker, Officer Jerry Baxter is going to run the prints for us if we drop them off. I asked her not to mention it to anyone else at the PD so hopefully her Sergeant won't find out about it until we catch the guy. She said she'd tell Baxter to keep mum too." Olivia reported happily.

"Awesome," Josh said, grinning at her enthusiasm. "Let's get going then. We can drop off the photos of the prints first. I'm going to call the realtor while we drive, if you don't mind driving."

"Not a problem," Olivia took her keys and her purse and headed toward the door. "At least the traffic seems to be good so far this morning."

"Yeah, the skiers all went to the slopes early, and I guess the shoppers haven't bothered to come out yet." Josh grabbed his parka and followed Olivia out, locking the door behind them.

"Speaking of skiing, we should take Emma and Sophia to the slopes again soon. Emma was really starting to get the hang of it last time and Sophia did great for her age too."

"Yes, we really should be getting out there more while they're little and it's so easy for them to learn new things." Josh agreed, opening the car door for Olivia. "As long as it's still cold enough for the resorts to blow snow, we should be taking every opportunity to ski with them. The season is almost over already."

"I think we can manage a couple of hours a day, three times a week without cutting into our working time right now, since we only have the one serious case at the moment." Olivia pulled the car into the road, "It's been a slow week so far, but that works in our favor for skiing."

"You're right. Let's make a date of it for the weekend for starters." Josh pulled his cell phone out of his parka pocket and reached to get the paper with the realtor's phone number on it from the other pocket. "I'll see if we can meet at the house you like later."

"That would be great," Olivia smiled. "I have to meet Abby, Julie, Pam and Vicki in town at some point tomorrow to check on the Bridesmaids and Maid of Honor dresses for the wedding. They will need to try their dresses on to see if any alterations are needed. My wedding dress may need some altering as well. You know I'm going to wear Mam's dress. I was hoping that she would be here before I needed to have it altered, but since they can't come until the week before the wedding, I can't wait. Too many things could go wrong."

"Yeah, Murphy's Law probably rules weddings," Josh chuckled. "I need to make sure Jimmy's tux is ready and fits him okay too, as well as Andrew's and Tiny's. It's a good thing Jimmy and Sally and James are living in the house in town now instead of out in Eastman's Grant. That makes life easier for everyone."

"Speaking of Eastman's Grant, I need to ask Abby if Tiny has said if he's going to make it back in time to be your Groomsman. You know, he was supposed to be out of town at some motorcycle thing, but should be back two days before the wedding if things go right." Olivia stopped at the police station.

"Okay, let me call the realtor quickly so we know our schedule," Josh grinned at Olivia's chatter.

"This is me, shutting up," Olivia laughed, as she jumped out to take the photos into the police station.

Josh chuckled as he dialed. He spoke into the phone for a few minutes while Olivia was inside, then disconnected looking pleased.

"We're on for two o'clock with the realtor," he informed Olivia with a satisfied smile when she got back in the car. "I had to talk her into it, because she really didn't want to show the house today. She said she'd planned to leave early to go shopping."

Olivia laughed, "You turned on that charm of yours and had her eating out of your hand, I'll bet. Wait until she sees how handsome you are. I'll have to fight to keep her off you."

Josh grinned, "You think I'm handsome, huh? Handsome enough to fight over? Hmmm, that's nice to know."

Olivia rolled her eyes laughingly. "You're such a guy," she teased him. "Watch, she's gonna be eighty and look like an elderly Olive Oyl. That'll teach you to charm women over the phone."

Josh laughed, "You're probably right on that. Hopefully, she'll at least be knowledgeable about the house and how much work it needs."

"Yes, I hope she is, and I hope the owner has disclosed all the problems it may have. It's a pretty house, at least the outside is and the location is perfect for our needs."

CHAPTER THREE

The snow banks on the sides of the road were a little higher on Candlewick Road, than on the more open town streets.

"It's looking more beautiful and feeling more like home every time we visit," Olivia sighed happily as they turned into the driveway of the stately old mansion which would soon be their new home. "Whoever Abby hired to do the exterior renovation and painting, has done a phenomenal job. I think it must look almost exactly the way it did back when James Hill's parents first lived here."

"They certainly have. It looks awesome." Josh parked at the top of the drive behind Abby's bright blue minivan. "If we don't have any more snow and the weather stays fairly nice, we may be able to have at least part of the wedding party outside after all. I know how much you wanted to do that originally."

"We were so lucky that we had such a warm spell this year or they'd never have been able to get this all done in time."

"Hey guys," Abby called to them from the front door with a huge grin on her face. "I can't wait to see what you think of the latest improvements."

Olivia and Josh gave her a hug as they entered the large and ornate foyer. Abby's normally cheerful face was beaming with obvious pride and delight as she waited to see their reactions.

Olivia gasped as her eyes traveled the length and breadth of the room, taking in the newly painted walls, the shining wooden stairs and banisters and the sunlight dancing in rich colors from the stained glass side lights onto the gleaming marble and granite floor. She recognized the stunning little Victorian loveseat with its delicately carved legs as having been here from the time she first saw the house. The Tiffany lamps were still sitting on the little Victorian table on the other side of the foyer as well. Everything had obviously been cleaned and polished thoroughly and looked so beautiful it almost brought tears to her eyes.

"Oh Abby, this is incredible," she cried, hugging her best friend again. "You are a magician!"

Abby's eyes shone with excitement. "Actually, Liv, the house and most of the furnishings were so perfect, they just needed some tender loving care to be exactly what I knew you wanted. It's an amazing house, and an antique lover's dream."

Olivia and Josh followed Abby up the right side of the U-shaped stairs, marveling at the highly polished wood of the stairs and railings. The huge crystal chandelier hanging over the foyer glistened as they passed it.

"That must have been a tough job all by itself," Olivia shook her head in amazement. "That poor chandelier was so covered in dust and cobwebs that we felt like we were in a Boris Karloff movie the last time we were here."

"Yes, it took some doing to get all the crystals totally clean," Abby chuckled. "My mom is the one who tackled that project. We had all the ceiling lamps and chandeliers taken down so she could clean them, then rehung afterward. She cleaned everything that was made of glass except for the windows."

"I hope you paid her from the expenses, but knowing Annie, I'm betting she wouldn't let you." Olivia remarked knowingly.

"Of course she wouldn't," Abby retorted. "You're like a second daughter to her. She wanted to do it for you."

Josh smiled with a slightly mischievous look on his face, "Well, we appreciate it enormously. Everything absolutely sparkles."

They moved on through the house, going room by room to see how lovely the old house had become under Abby's direction. Every bedroom was beautifully done, with the existing antique furniture cleaned and polished, and new mattresses and bedding on the beds. The antique Persian rugs which had been too mouse eaten to restore had been replaced with beautiful new Persian rugs that could stand up to being walked on. Abby had ordered it from a shop in town.

The master bedroom was beautiful and Olivia thought it was decorated perfectly for her and Josh. The diamond shaped window with a scalloped spoked wheel paned glass that rose above the head of the polished teak four poster bed was stunning now that it had been cleaned. The blue and white toile bedding matched the gorgeous new wallpaper with old fashioned scenes that somehow reminded Olivia of the scenes found on Wedgwood

Jasperware, except that these were more like early American rather than Greco-Roman.

Abby had redone the smaller bedroom that adjoined their room as a nursery, which it probably had once been before becoming a guest room. It now contained a beautiful antique iron spindle crib in a creamy white color.

"I found a couple real antique cribs that I thought you'd like the look of, but I couldn't find one that was in good enough condition that I liked well enough, so I had this one made by a company that makes antique looking cribs. It is almost an exact replica of the one I thought you'd like the best." Abby explained. "You know the nightstand and dresser that match it so well, are authentic antiques, and to me, without super close scrutiny, the crib looks the same age."

"They really do all look antique," Olivia put her hand over her heart. "They are so beautiful, Abby. It's even better than I could have imagined it."

The light teal and creamy white bedding and curtains were perfect for Sophia with her red hair and blue eyes, Olivia thought.

A beautiful sturdy looking hand carved antique wooden rocking horse that Olivia recognized from her visit to the little playhouse in the woods stood ready for Sophia to ride.

"You can't imagine how happy I am right now." Olivia hugged Abby again, then hugged Josh, holding him tight for a moment as tears of joy filled her eyes.

"Well, I think *I* can imagine it," Josh breathed against her hair. "I think I feel pretty much the same as you do."

Abby beamed, "Okay, now I'm happy too. I so wanted everything to be just the way you'd like it."

"It's perfect, Abs," Olivia smiled through her tears, "No one but you could have gotten everything to be the way I'd pictured it. In fact, it's even better. That gorgeous teal is so much nicer than the pale blue I'd imagined. Sophia will love it when she's old enough to appreciate it."

Olivia stepped back, and wiped her eyes and grinned, "Okay, let's see the rest."

They walked through the music room, oohing and ahhing over the newly polished baby grand piano that had featured prominently in a case Olivia and Josh had solved a few months before, then out onto the balcony with its brand-new boards, railings and fresh paint.

The back yard was still holding a small amount of untouched snow and the effect combined with the woods in the background was lovely.

They opened the glass swinging door to enter the little hallway that led to the other bedrooms and back to the large staircase they'd ascended earlier. Abby opened the door to the first bedroom on their right, and proudly displayed the job she'd done restoring the sweet bedroom that Olivia had chosen for Emma.

The lovely antique white canopy bed was made up with fresh green and white ivy patterned bedding with a green skirt and a filmy white canopy billowing down gracefully from each corner. The antique white dresser Olivia had found matched beautifully, and Olivia knew the sweet doll sitting on the bed would thrill Emma. The matching antique wardrobe reminded Olivia so much of the Wardrobe in the Chronicles of Narnia, that she knew Emma would be enthralled.

"Oh Abby, she's going to love it!" Olivia bounced up and down in her excitement for her ward. "You totally rocked everything! I can't wait for her to see it."

Abby sighed happily. "Okay, the only things I haven't finished with are the summerhouse and the playhouse. I need your input on how you want them to be."

"Wow, Abby, I'm really awed at how fabulous this all is. I couldn't have done it nearly as well." Olivia threw her arms out as if embracing the whole house. "Let's see the other five bedrooms and the rest of the downstairs, then we'll take a look at the summerhouse and playhouse."

The other rooms were all just as wonderfully renovated as the ones they'd seen and Josh and Olivia were overjoyed. It was everything they'd imagined it could be and more.

The cute little summerhouse just inside the woods had been thoroughly cleaned and aired out with fresh paint on the exterior. The shingle roof had been replaced, the many windows sparkled and it was ready for Olivia and Josh to choose the interior color and furnishings.

"I love the grey shingles with the white wood," Olivia remarked. "I think I'd like to go with white furniture and maybe light blue and white cushions. What about a nice glider rocker, a small table and a loveseat, with a throw rug in the center? I think it is probably better to go with new furniture in here, as it won't have heat and air conditioning, so wouldn't be the best atmosphere for antiques. Abby, the whitewashed oak hardwood floor is awesome. The floor was so covered in dust when I last saw it that I couldn't even tell what it was made of. Did you have to replace it or just refinish it?"

"It had to be replaced. They trashed the summerhouse pretty bad when Salger and his gang were using it as a hideout." Abby grimaced, "There were deep gouges in the floor that no amount of refinishing could fix. Your furniture ideas are great. I agree about the new versus antique for the same reasons. It's amazing that most of the antiques in the main house survived so well for all those years without any climate control at all, but there's no sense in pushing it."

"I think just plain white for the interior walls as well, don't you?" Olivia asked Josh and Abby.

They both nodded.

"It sounds like it will be a nice place to just relax and read or doze in the summertime. Attractive and comfortable, with plenty of windows and enough shade from the trees to be pleasant." Josh agreed. "I can easily see us spending time here with the kids."

"Okay, that's settled then," Abby nodded, as if checking off another thing on the list in her head. "On to the playhouse."

The adorable little playhouse was nestled a little bit further into the woods to give it a feeling of separateness, like it was another property entirely.

It was a little wood-sided cabin with a single large room in the front and two tiny rooms in the back. Abby had hired someone to clean it thoroughly and it was so different from how it looked the last time Olivia had seen it that she could barely recognize it.

All of the old vintage and antique toys and sports equipment that had been stored there, except for the rocking horse that now resided in Sophia's room, were gathered in the main room awaiting Olivia and Josh to decide their fate.

Josh and Olivia were both practically dancing in delight over the wonderful toys. There were antique wooden sleds, fabulous antique skis, various antique pull toys as well as numerous vintage toys and skis which were probably used by the Hill children, Jenny and James, the last people to live in the house.

"Oooh," Josh croaked in an awed voice, "This old Lionel train set is unreal. It's got to be from the 1930's or earlier."

"Let me see," Olivia cried excitedly. "My Da collects old trains." She lifted the engine car reverently, "This looks like it's from the early 1920's. Da will flip when he sees it."

"Then it will be our belated Christmas gift to him," Josh grinned. "I had no idea what to get your folks, so that takes care of your Da, at least."

"He'll be thrilled. I don't think we could have found anything he'd like better."

"Look at this dollhouse!" Olivia gasped. "Emma and Sophia both will love this, at least Sophia will when she's older. It's incredible."

Abby helped Olivia lift the drop cloth all the way off the huge handmade Victorian style dollhouse so they could see it better.

"I thought you'd want it for the girls, but I didn't know if you wanted it to stay in the playhouse or be moved into Emma's room for now."

Abby and Josh watched as Olivia sank to her knees entranced.

"Hmm, maybe I should have put it in your room, Liv," Abby joked, "If I'd known how much you were going to like it, I would have."

"It's amazing," Olivia breathed, moving the little family from one room to another, touching the beautiful handmade wooden furniture. "Even the wooden shingles on the roof are handmade. This is the most beautiful dollhouse I've ever seen."

"They even have a dog and a cat," Josh chuckled, picking up the tiny hand painted animals. "There is also a mother, a father, a little girl, a little boy and a baby. This could almost be our family, Livvie, except that we don't have a little boy, and Sophia is older than this baby."

"This is so cool," Olivia grinned like a happy child. "I think we should put it in Emma's room for now, then when she's older and Sophia is old enough to play with it, we can move it to her room. Sophia is too young for all these small pieces right now. She puts everything in her mouth."

"That sounds like a plan," Josh agreed. "Emma will love it."

"The old pull toys all seem to be in fairly good shape and I think we can let Sophia play with most of them, though there are a couple here that really look like they should be on display somewhere instead of being used."

Olivia gently pulled a very old looking toy horse on a platform with wheels away from the group of toys, "This horse looks like it's from the late 1800's to early 1900's and is definitely too fragile to be played with anymore."

"I'd thought of putting it in the library to use as part of the décor, but wasn't sure if you wanted to try to use it for the kids," Abby smiled. "It would look pretty awesome on top of the mantle, though."

"Yes it would," Josh agreed as Olivia nodded her approval.

"I think we should fix up the playhouse like a real house for Emma and Sophia to pretend it's their house. We can make a tiny kitchen and a bedroom out of the two small rooms and the big room can be the living room and dining room. They can play and have tea parties and all kinds of fun things," Olivia's voice was dreamy. "I'd have loved this when I was a little girl."

"I'll bet Emma and Sophia will too," Josh put his arm around her shoulders. "We can keep all the sports equipment and things like that in the basement in the house. The antique sleds and things like that can be used to decorate the house, if they fit anywhere."

"Great idea, Josh," Olivia leaned into him for a moment. "Okay, Abby, do you think you can find some nice child sized furnishing for the playhouse?"

"You guys don't want antiques, right?"

"No, just pretty things that will make it look homey and fun for them." Olivia smiled.

"Preferably nothing plastic though. Make it look like a real home in miniature." Josh interjected.

"Since the playhouse has natural cedar walls, you don't need to worry about painting. I'll grab a few little throw rugs for the wood floors and look for the furniture, so it will be a cozy little play-home, not just a playhouse then." Abby smiled brightly. "I'll move the antiques up to the main house and we can figure out where you want them and decide what to do with whatever you don't want to keep."

They headed back to the house, with Abby carrying the little wooden horse for the library. Josh carried the train set in its wooden box for Olivia's father and Olivia carried a pair of old wooden skis, which she thought would look great hanging in the den.

"Abby," Josh called, "Do you know when they will have the fence finished? I know it hasn't been easy with the ground frozen, but I want to make sure it is safe for Molly before we move in. She's very good about not running off, but even so, it isn't safe for her without a fence."

"The contractor said he'll have it completed by Monday as long as the weather stays nice," Abby said over her shoulder. "The electrician will have to connect the motor for the gate when he's done, but that will be quick."

"You've done an amazing job with all of this Abby," Josh praised her. "You could put general contractors out of business."

"It's been challenging, but a lot of fun too," she replied as they entered the house. "Having an unlimited budget was a big plus. It wouldn't have been quite as much fun if I had to pinch pennies on it."

"Oh, Josh, it's almost time to meet the realtor," Olivia gasped, glancing at her watch. "Abby, we've got to run or we'll be late."

"Realtor?" Abby looked surprised. "You're selling your old house, Liv? I thought Julie was going to live there."

"She is. No, this is for an office. I'll tell you all about it later." Olivia hugged her friend. "You rock Abby. Everything you've done here is perfect!"

"It really is, Abby," Josh hugged her too, as they headed for the front door. "Let me know if there is anything you need."

"I will, Josh, but I think I have it all under control for now." She laughed and put the back of her hand to her forehead dramatically, "Whew! The end is in sight. Call me, Liv."

"I will," Olivia called back as they hurried to the SUV.

CHAPTER FOUR

"Wow, I can't believe it's so late. It didn't seem like we were here that long, did it?"

"Not even close," Josh agreed. "It's okay, we'll make it on time."

He turned the vehicle around and drove down the long curving driveway. They looked at the tall black wrought iron picket fence that was mostly completed near the entrance.

"The fence will be a nice aesthetic touch besides the safety aspect of it, I think," he commented, looking at the arrow finials on top, with an arch rising over the top of every other arrow. It's as close to the original old fence as you could ask for, but without the rust. If you don't want to sell them to one of your clients, or use them in some way, I was thinking we could give the old antique fence panels to Abby to either sell or use in her decorating business. What do you think?"

"There are some that are in pretty decent shape considering their age. That's a great idea. She'll be very happy to have them." Olivia thought for a moment, "I may save one to use in the kitchen. I can hang it horizontally from the ceiling and use it to hang copper pots and dry herbs by hanging them there too. It will give it an interesting flair."

"Sounds cool," Josh smiled as he steered the SUV off of Candlewick Road into the main road. "Sounds a little witchy and mysterious too. Like something you'd find in an old medieval kitchen or a witch's cottage from a fairy tale."

"Exactly," Olivia grinned, "An old slightly spooky mansion needs to have something like that just to intrigue visitors and make them wonder."

"Livvie, I have an idea," Josh's lips twisted up in a quirky smile. "You know how Annie and Abby, especially Annie, are always doing things for us and not wanting to accept payment? What about if we send them on a one week vacation, all expenses paid to somewhere nice and warm, like a tropical island. Would they go?"

Olivia's mouth dropped open. "Are you kidding? Of course they'd go. We'd have to tell them it was all paid for and non-cancellable, but they would be ecstatic!" She shook her head, laughing, "They'll be head-over-heels-happy."

Josh laughed, "I'm glad to hear that. It was hard to come up with something I thought they'd like. We can present them with it when we get back from our honeymoon."

It was just before two o'clock when Josh pulled into the driveway of the house Olivia had spotted that morning. The realtor was sitting in a small blue car waiting for them.

They quickly got out and met her on the front porch, shaking hands and thanking her for meeting with them on short notice.

Olivia's eyes twinkled mischievously as she shook hands with the tall, rail thin seventyish woman. Olive Oyl had been a fairly accurate guess. She was careful not to look at Josh lest she break out in giggles.

The realtor, Hannah Pine, was very nice and seemed to be well informed about the property, as well as honest enough to not be hiding flaws that she knew about.

Josh and Olivia followed her through the house, which was still furnished with wonderful vintage furniture that Olivia gauged to be from the 1940s and 1950s, trying to picture it as the office/living quarters they needed.

Josh stopped abruptly, and Olivia, who had been looking at the bay window, walked right into him.

"Sorry," he laughed, after making sure she hadn't hurt herself by hitting his back with her face, "I just had a crazy and maybe wonderful idea."

"Okay, let's hear it," Olivia laughed, smoothing her hair down after the brush with Josh's parka.

"Remember how I wanted to figure out a way for you to have your own little antique shop? Well, why aren't we thinking of making part of this house, or whichever one we end up with, into your antique shop? We can have both businesses in the same building, as well as having a couple of rooms for relaxing with the kids and for whoever is babysitting to hang out in."

"Josh, that's an awesome idea!" Olivia bounced up and down on her toes. "I've always wanted to have my own little shop."

"Now you're going to have to think of a name for it," Josh laughed. "Remember how long it took us to come up with MVI, Mountain Valley Investigations? And that isn't even very original since a couple of other businesses have Mountain Valley in the name."

"Oh boy," Olivia laughed, "You're right. This will take a lot of thought. But I'm so excited."

The realtor listened to their conversation with a smile, "How do you think this house would work so far?"

"Well, we haven't looked at anything else at all yet, but from what I've seen, it is looking pretty good," Josh assured her. "We'll be able to tell you more once we've seen the whole house."

They followed her up the stairs to see the three bedrooms and full bathroom contained up there.

"What if we converted the upstairs into a nice place for the kids and used all of the downstairs except for the family room for the antique shop? The family room is large and looks perfect for the MVI office." Josh watched Olivia's face for clues to how she felt about it.

Her eyes shone, "Josh, I think it's all exactly right. I can picture it just the way you described. We might have to keep the kitchen free from the antique shop so we can make lunch, but if I can use the living room and dining room for the shop, it will be just what I need."

"Do we need to look at any other houses?" Josh asked, glancing at the hopeful look on the realtor's face.

"I don't if you don't," Olivia answered with a huge smile. "If there aren't any issues with the property that we don't know of, I'd say it's exactly what we're looking for."

"The only thing I know of that might be an issue is that some people think the house is haunted, because one of the owners was murdered here a very long time ago," the woman confided, looking like she'd rather not have to disclose that particular piece of information, "You're not the superstitious sort, are you?"

Olivia and Josh reassured her that they wouldn't refuse to make an offer because of that, though Olivia had a look in her eyes that Josh knew all too well.

"Did they arrest the murderer?" she asked.

"No, they were never able to figure out who had killed him. It was fifty years ago though, so there's certainly no need to worry if the killer is still around."

Josh suppressed a grin, knowing that he and Olivia would soon be looking into a fifty-year-old murder in their spare time.

Josh talked to the realtor about the price and what she thought they should offer, while Olivia wandered through the house again, checking closets, and making sure everything looked like it was in reasonably good shape. She didn't want any nasty surprises once they started remodeling.

She finished touring the house and since Josh and Hannah Pine were still deep in discussion over the price and closing costs and such, she wandered outside to scope out the back yard.

There were a few spots with snow still sitting on the lawn, but mostly it had melted off, so she knew the yard must get a fair amount of sun, so the grass and plants should grow nicely in the summer. She could hear the river close by, and decided to see if the property actually touched it behind the border of trees in the back.

Olivia was pleased to discover that the river was very close, so it was likely that the property did include river frontage. She headed back inside to ask Hannah about it.

Josh was looking pleased, and Hannah looked even happier than Josh.

"Hannah, does the house have any river frontage attached?" Olivia asked.

Hanna smiled brightly, "Yes, it has two hundred feet of river frontage."

"What do you think, Liv?" Josh asked. "Do we need to think about it for a while, or are you ready to make an offer?"

"I love it, so it is up to you now," Olivia answered. "What do you think?"

"I love it too, so I guess we're making an offer now," he directed the second half of the sentence to Hannah Pine.

"That's great," Hannah replied, juggling her folders. "If you can come back to my office, I can write it up and get your signatures and present it to Bill and Elisa Brown, who are the owners."

"Yes, I think we can do that, if it isn't going to take too long. When do you think the owners will want to close?"

"I'm sure they would be delighted to close as soon as possible. They need the money pretty badly, since I think they are hurting from having to pay all those medical bills for Bill's heart surgery. His health insurance had lapsed and they were so distraught from his recent heart attacks that they didn't realize it until they started getting huge bills from the hospital." Hannah locked the door behind them, as they walked out. "I think they owe almost as much as they're asking for the house." She stopped abruptly, as if realizing that she might not have been wise to share that with potential buyers, since it could cause them to drop the offering price.

"We are getting married in four weeks, so we definitely wouldn't need to close before the wedding. There's way too much to do for that, and we want to have our names on the deed as a married couple," Josh smiled. "Will they mind waiting a few weeks? I know the Browns. They are very trustworthy and I'm really sorry to hear that they'd had such a bad time lately. We can give them a deposit upfront, rather than holding it in escrow."

"Congratulations," Hannah gushed. "It's always nice to have newlyweds buying a house from me. It seems like a good omen. I'm positive they won't mind waiting as long as it isn't too long, especially if you're willing to hand over a deposit now. I imagine you could even start with your renovations now if you wanted to, as long as your deposit is given and the contract signed."

They followed her back and Josh wrote down the offer on a piece of paper which he passed to Hannah. Her eyes widened as she read it, and she glanced at Josh, as if asking if she'd read it correctly. He gave her a faint nod with a smile. Olivia and Josh waited while she typed up the contract. Once it had been signed, she emailed it to the sellers, and called them to make sure they saw it.

They sent it back signed almost before the ink had dried on Josh's and Olivia's signatures. Josh wrote out a check for the Browns for a deposit and they thanked Hannah for her assistance. She thanked them heartily for their purchase, assuring them that she'd be in touch so they could schedule the closing.

Once Olivia and Josh were seated in the SUV, Olivia turned to Josh.

"I saw the look on her face when she read the offer," her eyebrows rose and her eyes held a twinkle. "You offered the full asking price, didn't you?"

Josh chuckled, "Yeah, she gave me away with that look. Bill and Elisa Brown are good hard working people, and Elisa's been working two jobs as well as taking care of Bill since he had the first heart attack." He sobered, "I hadn't really realized how badly they needed money. I didn't know his insurance hadn't covered his medical bills. I made the offer for twenty-thousand-dollars over the asking price. They actually had it priced quite a bit lower than they should to try to sell it quickly. I've also decided that I am going to pay his medical bills in full. He's too proud to take charity, but I will do it anonymously, so he can't refuse."

"If you've ever wondered why I love you so much, this is a prime example," Olivia hugged him. "You are the most caring person I know."

"Lots of people care, and I'm sure many would love to do what I'm doing. I just happen to be lucky enough to be able to afford to do it," Josh said modestly. "That's the only difference."

"Well, I know better than that, but I'm certainly not going to argue with you about it," she smiled, leaning her head against his chest as he started the engine.

"I guess we should stop at the PD to see what Officer Baxter found, if anything." Josh turned the car in that direction. "Why don't we stop and pick up some pizzas from the Flatbread Place on the way to get the girls after the PD? It's been a long day and I'm sure you feel as little like cooking as I do."

"Oh, that sounds wonderful. They've got such good pizza. Emma and Sophia will be happy as well. Molly and Sheyna will have to get a bite too, you know, so we'd better get two. "I'll call the order in so it's ready when we get there."

Josh laughed, "I'm really hungry tonight, so we'd definitely better get two. It's a good thing we all have the same favorite."

"Sheyna and Molly are a lot more into the goat's cheese than the rest of it though," Olivia grinned. "That's my least favorite part, so it works out great for all three of us."

"Remember Sophia's face the first time she tasted the goat's cheese?"

"It was almost as priceless as the first time we gave her a pickle when she was cutting a bottom molar." Olivia laughed. "I wish we'd had a cell phone handy to video tape it."

Josh pulled into the police station's little parking area and they hopped out together.

Julie was in the building writing up a report when they stepped inside.

"Jerry ran the prints, but unfortunately, they weren't in the system. I made copies of these for you, and we're going to keep the originals so we have them when he's caught." Julie greeted them. "I guess that means that either he's good at not getting caught or he just started running cons recently."

"I hope it's the latter," Josh said dryly. "I want him off the streets before he cons anyone else."

"We're going to pick up pizza from the Flatbread Place for dinner, Jules, are you going to be home to eat with us?" Olivia took the envelope Julie handed her with the photocopies in it.

"Ooh, now that I know what we're having I will be there for sure," Julie grinned. "Best pizza ever."

Josh laughed as he started the car, "Okay, let's make that three pizzas."

Olivia giggled as his stomach rumbled with the thought of the mouthwatering pizza. "It's a good thing I called it in. I'm not sure your tummy could wait too much longer."

"I told you I was hungry," Josh grinned. "I'll run in and grab it if you don't want to get out."

"That works for me. I can call Annie and let her know we're on the way."

Olivia made the quick call while Josh went to pay for the pizza.

Josh got in hurriedly, handing the pizza boxes to Olivia, since they were going to need the rest of the SUV for the kids and animals.

"Ooh, that pizza smells so good, I may wish we'd ordered even more," Olivia groaned. "The garlic smell is going to be torture until we can eat."

Josh laughed as her stomach growled even louder than his had.

Annie had the kids all bundled up and ready to go, and Molly and Sheyna pranced excitedly around their humans, waiting for their rear door to be opened.

After hugging Annie and coercing her into letting them pay her, they put Molly and Sheyna in their crates and got Emma and Sophia into their car seats, and quickly buckled themselves in to drive to Olivia's house.

Once Molly and Sheyna had eaten, the humans' dinner was a happy and festive meal, with both children digging into the pizza with gusto, even though little Sophia managed to wear almost as much as she ate. Julie was home when they arrived and in between talking with Emma and Sophia, the adults shared all their news of the day.

"I am so happy that the house is looking so good. Is it really going to be ready for you to move in right after the wedding?"

"It looks that way, yes," Josh answered swallowing a bite of pizza hastily. "Except for the fence not being quite finished, we could even move in right now. The main house is basically finished."

"I can't wait to see it," Julie enthused. "By the way, Livvie, I would love it if you could talk to your friend, Pam to see if there are any new people moving into the retirement home that need a new home for their pets. If you're still okay with it, I am ready to adopt either a dog or a cat, and would love to be involved in your visiting animal program."

"That's awesome, Jules," Olivia beamed. "The program has been doing really well. We have several volunteers that can bring the former owner to visit his or her pet if you'd rather not have to pick them up now and then."

"I don't mind picking them up at all. How often will they visit and what days? My schedule is not terribly flexible, as you know."

"It shouldn't be a problem to adjust it to work with your schedule. It's a wonderful thing you're doing, Julie."

"It's partly selfish. I really miss having pets, but I know how hard it must be for these people to not be allowed to bring their pets into the retirement home with them." Julie smiled crookedly, "It gives me a warm and fuzzy feeling to be able to do this for someone."

"That's because you're a warm and fuzzy person," Olivia hugged her friend. "I'll give Pam a call tomorrow."

"Oops!" Josh jumped up as Emma accidentally knocked her milk over into his lap. "Well, that woke me up," he laughed, picking up the glass, as Olivia ran for a towel to mop up the milk. She handed one to Josh who wiped his pants, ruffling Emma's hair with his other hand.

"I'm sorry, Uncle Josh," Emma said sadly, with a little tear forming in her eye. "It was an accident."

"I know, sweetie. It's nothing to worry about. Everybody has accidents sometimes."

She sniffled and a smile broke through her tears. "I love you, Uncle Josh."

"I love you too, Emma," Josh hugged the little girl and kissed her forehead.

"I'll get you some more milk, Ems," Olivia smiled, patting the child's head on the way to the kitchen.

"Thank you, Aunt Livvie. I love you too," Emma said happily when Olivia returned with a new glass of milk.

"And I love you more, Pumpkin," Olivia hugged her. "Finish up your dinner sweetie. It's getting late and you need to go to bed soon. Look at Sophia, she's almost asleep in her food."

Josh laughed as Olivia picked Sophia up and carried her upstairs to bathe her and put her to bed.

"Goodnight Sweetpea!" he called to Sophia.

"Night Daddy," Sophia responded sleepily.

"Goodnight Sophia," Emma jumped up to kiss her sister.

"Night Emma," Sophia smeared pizza sauce on her sister's face as she kissed her back.

Josh wiped Emma's face as she sat back down.

Emma finished her food before Olivia returned from putting Sophia to bed, and gave everyone goodnight kisses, then went upstairs to get ready for bed.

"Wow," Josh chuckled to Julie, "She must be sleepy. She didn't even ask if she could stay up longer."

"It is a bit later than you usually eat. You guys had a long day today, and I'll bet Annie played with them a lot so they got all tired out." Julie laughed. "They should sleep soundly tonight."

"I'm sure they will," Josh agreed, getting up to feed Molly and Sheyna a few treats.

"I'm headed to bed myself," Julie yawned, helping Josh to carry the dishes into the kitchen. "I know it's early for me, but I'm starting to study for my Sergeant's exam. Not that I'm planning to take it right away . . . not until next year at least, but I want to know it all really well by then, so I've been studying every chance I get."

"That's a great idea. You are definitely Sergeant material Julie. If you ever need any help with it, let me know." Josh offered. "See you tomorrow." He turned to the sink to rinse the dishes before putting them in the dishwasher.

As soon as he'd turned the machine on, he went upstairs to kiss the children goodnight. At the doorway of the room Emma and Sophia were sharing, he stood entranced by the sweet picture of Olivia sitting on Emma's bed holding the sleeping Sophia in one arm and a children's book in the other hand, while reading to Emma in a soft voice.

He waited until she'd finished and Emma was drifting off to sleep, then bent and kissed her forehead gently, pulling the blanket up to her shoulders. Olivia kissed

Emma, then rose carefully and placed Sophia in her crib, covering her with her little quilt. They both kissed Sophia and tiptoed to the door. Olivia turned off the light, leaving only a dim nightlight to chase away the dark.

They stood in the doorway, arm in arm for a moment, watching the children sleep, then walked quietly downstairs to the living room to sit by the fire.

"Oh Josh, I am so excited about the wedding, but it's stressing me out too," Olivia moaned, sinking into the couch. "There is so much to do and not nearly enough time to get it done."

"We need to find someone to help Abby with it. She's been so busy with the house that she doesn't have enough time for both either." Josh sighed. "Your folks will be here in three weeks and things will be even more hectic, right?"

"Actually, I think Mam will be able to help with everything. She's really good at getting things done. Nana's not bad either, but she can't get around as well as she used to since her knee replacement, and she has a pretty strong Irish brogue, so I doubt she'd do well on the phone either," Olivia giggled. "She'd have a rough time getting people to understand her.

"When is Peter coming up?" Olivia asked about Josh's dad. "Will he be able to stay for at least a few days before the wedding? I know he and Da and Pop will get along famously."

"I think he'll be here the day after your folks get here, but he'll be staying in my apartment with me, so you have enough room for your folks." Josh put his arm around her, "I offered to let him and your folks stay at Candlewick, but they all refused. They want us to be the first to live in it since the renovation."

"We have awesome parents." Olivia leaned her head against his shoulder. "We have some pretty awesome kids too."

Josh sighed, "Yes we do. I am really worried about how it will be if we ever find Emma's biological family. The PD on Mary's Orchard, and the local PD here, as well as the state police have all come up empty." I ran her picture, approximate age and fingerprints through every missing person's database available and haven't had a single hit."

"I think her real first name probably is Emma, as it seems to be so natural to her to offer it. Every time I've tried asking her about her last name, she hesitates before she tells me it is Harmon, as if she's almost remembering what it used to be before she was abducted and told to use her kidnappers' last name." Olivia said sadly. "I keep thinking that one of these days, she's going to just blurt out her real last name from somewhere back in her subconscious memory, and then we'll be able to figure out where she came from. Part of me hopes that'll happen and the rest of me dreads it."

"I know. I feel the same way." Josh hugged her. "I really wish we could adopt her as well as Sophia, but until we can figure out whether she has parents who want her back, I don't see that happening. At least we have temporary guardianship, and the judge will give us first dibs on adopting her when the time comes."

"I want what's best for her, but as altruistic as I try to be, I'm selfishly hoping that it's best for her for us to be able to adopt her somehow." Olivia admitted. "I love her so much that it would be horrible to have to give her up."

Molly snuggled her head into Olivia's lap as if to comfort her, and Olivia hugged her.

"Molly, you're always so in tune with my feelings. I couldn't do without you."

Sheyna meowed from the back of the couch behind their heads, and Josh reach back and picked her up, setting her in his lap to pet her. She proceeded to knead his jeans, while purring loudly.

"I'm going to put her in Emma's bed tonight and see if she'll stay. Emma was asking if she'd sleep with her." Olivia rubbed behind Sheyna's ears. "How about it, Sheyna? How'd you like to make Emma happy?"

"I should get going," Josh yawned, stretching and causing Sheyna to leap from his lap in annoyance. "Sorry Sheyna. Tomorrow is going to be another long day."

"Yes, I think every day is going to be pretty full until after the wedding," Olivia chuckled, rubbing his shoulders. "You know I probably won't be able to work in the office or on the case much tomorrow, since I have to meet Abby, Vicki, Pam and Julie for dress fittings. Sophia and Emma have to have their last fittings done too. I think that will take quite a lot of time."

"I had a feeling you would be occupied most of the day, so I planned to try to do some leg work on the con man, as well as finishing up the paperwork on the Oswald case, so we can submit the bill and put it away." Josh smiled as he stood up, "I have a few people in the lakes area that I want to interview in case they saw the con artist around. I don't need you for that, so it works out perfectly."

Molly followed Olivia and Josh to the front door, nuzzling Josh's hand for goodbye pets, and he bent to hug her.

"Take care of everyone, Molly. You're in charge," he kissed her on the nose and rose to kiss Olivia goodbye. "Call me when you have time, and I'll see you for dinner, okay?"

"Definitely," Olivia kissed him back. "I hope you get some good leads from your interviews."

As she closed and locked the door behind him, Molly pushed her head against Olivia's hand and headed for the back door. Olivia laughed and followed her obediently.

"Okay Mols, go do your thing," she opened the back door and stepped onto the deck to wait for Molly to conduct her nightly business with nature.

It was a clear night and the moon shone brightly overhead, illuminating the back yard, and casting shadows on the wooden deck. Olivia breathed in deeply, pulling the fresh mountain air into her lungs. Everything would work out the way it should, she told herself, letting go of her worries and feeling a sense of calm settle over her like a comforting blanket.

CHAPTER FIVE

Olivia hurried to get the little girls dressed and fed the next morning, so they wouldn't be late to meet her friends for the dress fitting.

She fed Molly and Sheyna and took Molly out in the back yard again before they left. They both seemed content to stay home after their day at Annie's yesterday.

Olivia loaded the children into their car seats after making sure she had a bottle for Sophia, who still liked her bottle at nap time, and extra snacks for both girls.

Abby, Pam and Vicki were already waiting at the bridal shop when they arrived and Julie pulled up in her police car before Olivia had even stepped out of the car.

She unbuckled Emma's car seat while Olivia got Sophia out of hers and they quickly joined Abby and Vicki inside.

The fittings went well, and they all agreed that Emma and Sophia were adorable in their little dresses with the big bows.

"I can't wait to see them with Molly and Sheyna, wearing their bows too," Vicki giggled. "It's gonna be so cute. Two little human girls and two little furry girls as flower girls."

"It couldn't get any cuter," Abby agreed, laughing. "I am so glad you chose colors that compliment redheads. Sophia, Molly and I would all have looked awful if you'd chosen one of those mauve or orange shades the shop owner was showing us in the beginning. The sage green and white looks great on everyone."

Julie had to leave to get back to work, but the others decided to have lunch at a little café in the next block where they could sit by the window and people watch.

Olivia gave Josh a quick call to see how his day was going then joined her friends and wards in conversation while they ate.

Once they'd finished and her friends had left, Olivia realized she still had plenty of time before she needed to go home, so she stopped the car at the library and took Emma and Sophia inside so she could do a little research.

She found a picture book for Sophia and a little first reader type book for Emma and put them together in a big comfortable chair beside hers while she looked up a fifty-year-old murder on microfilm.

"Aunt Livvie, what's this word?" Emma pointed to a spot in her book.

"Bobbing," Olivia answered with a smile. "It means they were trying to bite into apples that were floating in water. That's a game some kids play on Halloween."

"Can we do that on Halloween?"

"I don't see why not," Olivia handed the book back. "It's quite a while before Halloween though, so you'll need to remind me when it gets closer, okay?"

"Okey dokey," Emma sat back happily.

"Okey dokey," Sophia repeated. "Okey dokey dokey."

Emma giggled and Sophia joined in.

Olivia chuckled as she went back to her research.

Her eyes were starting to get tired from studying the reels of microfilm when her cell phone rang, showing Josh as the caller.

"Whew, you saved my poor eyes," she answered. "I've been scanning microfilm for the past hour and I can't see straight anymore."

"What are you looking up, the old murder?" Josh asked teasingly.

"You really do know me well, don't you?" Olivia laughed. "Yes, that's exactly what I've been doing. I found out the victim's name, age and occupation, but so far, I really haven't found anything exciting, and I've looked at almost everything from that whole time period."

"Well, I guess the next step is to see who we can find that was around back then and see if they remember anything we don't already know."

"Are you back from the Lakes Region yet? I'm going to wrap up here and head home. Sophia is starting to get as tired and cranky as my eyes."

"Yeah, I'm already in North Conway, so as soon as I make a stop at the gas station to fill up, I'll head toward your house. I'm bringing Italian food for dinner."

"Josh, you are truly a wonderful man," Olivia laughed. "I was already thinking about how much I didn't want to cook tonight."

"I'm feeling pretty much the same, so I stopped off for food already, and it smells good, so head on home and I'll meet you there soon."

Olivia was smiling as she closed the microfilm reader and bundled Emma and Sophia up in their coats and mittens. Emma dressed herself, but still had trouble with her zippers once in a while.

The air was still warm for the season, so Olivia didn't bother with her own hat. The cool breeze blew away her tiredness as she carried the sleeping Sophia to the car.

"Emma, Uncle Josh brought you and Sophia spaghetti for dinner. Are you hungry?"

"Yes, I am very hungry," Emma giggled. "My tummy is mad. It sounds like I have a lion in there. It says 'Feed me. Feed me.'"

Olivia tickled her as she fastened the buckles on her car seat. "We will get you and your lion fed quickly then, right?"

"Right!" Emma agreed giggling hysterically. "I am so ticklish, Aunt Livvie."

"You sure are, Emma," Olivia laughed as she ruffled Emma's hair and closed the back door.

The clock on the dashboard read 5:00 when Olivia pulled into her driveway, parking next to Josh's smaller SUV.

She helped Emma unbuckle, then carried Sophia into the house. Josh met her at the door and lifted Emma into the air, hugging her and twirling her around in a circle.

"How's my Emma?" he asked. "Are you ready to play airplane?"

"Hi Uncle Josh!" she shouted happily. "I am *so* ready to play airplane. That's the most funnest game ever."

He grinned and flew her around the living room, holding her with one strong arm under her stomach and the other holding her ankles. She held her back straight and her arms out to the side mimicking and airplane and they both made whooshing, roaring noises.

Olivia watched, laughing and occasionally dodging when Emma's outstretched arms came too close. Sophia woke up with a cry and Olivia bounced her gently, speaking soothingly until she woke up all the way.

Sophia watched her sister flying in the air for a couple of minutes, then sniffed back her tears and said "Airpane Daddy. I wanna pay airpane."

"Okay, Sophia, it's your turn to play," Josh slowed Emma's forward motion and gently lowered her to the floor on her belly.

She giggled and jumped up. "Sophia, you're gonna be the airplane now. Fly over my head."

Josh lifted Sophia and repeated his flying routine with her. She laughed and reached to try to touch Emma as she passed over her head.

"Wook, Emma. I fy too," she exclaimed proudly.

Josh flew her around for a couple more minutes then slowly lowered her to the floor beside Emma. "Okay, girls, time to get ready for dinner."

Emma took Sophia's hand and led her to the downstairs bathroom to wash her hands for dinner.

Josh kissed Olivia and they hugged for a moment in easy silence.

Molly woofed a greeting, and now that it seemed safe to walk around, Sheyna wound her way between Olivia's and Josh's legs, asking to be picked up.

Olivia and Josh knelt to pet Molly, and Sheyna hopped to her favorite spot on Josh's shoulders.

"And how are my furry girls tonight?" Olivia rubbed Molly with one hand and reached up to rub Sheyna's head, as she leaned down from Josh's shoulders to rub against Olivia's head. "How would you like a walk?"

Molly woofed her enthusiasm and ran to get their harnesses and leads. Sheyna purred as she waited for her dog and human servants to get her ready for her walk.

Josh laughed, as he took the harnesses from Molly's mouth and put Sheyna's on her while Olivia put Molly's on. "I'll let the kids help me set the table and we'll be ready for you when you get back."

"Well girls, it's a nice night for walking, but I'm hungry so let's make it a brisk walk. What do you say?"

Molly and Sheyna ignored her question and walked at their normal pace, stopping to sniff at exciting smells occasionally.

Olivia grinned and sighed, "Yeah, that's what I thought you'd say."

Emma and Sophia were sitting at the table and Josh was opening the take out bags with the containers of Italian food when Olivia walked into the kitchen. Molly and Sheyna hurried over and dug into their bowls which Josh had filled with their dinner.

"Thanks for getting everyone fed tonight, Josh." Olivia hugged him as he took one of the containers out of the bag. "I stayed at the library a bit longer than I'd planned."

"No problem, Liv," Josh carried two of the containers to the table as Olivia grabbed the other two. "You feed us all more often than I do."

"Mama, I hungry," Sophia announced firmly.

"That's good sweetie, because Daddy brought you spaghetti for supper. I know you and Emma like spaghetti, right?" Olivia spooned some spaghetti into a small bowl for her.

"Tank 'ou." Sophia said politely, jabbing her spoon into the spaghetti and smearing some of it on her chin as she took a bite.

"You're welcome Pumpkin," Olivia ruffled her hair as she wiped her mouth with a napkin. "You have peaches for dessert too."

"Yummy," Emma cried happily. "I love peaches."

"Aunt Annie canned these peaches herself and gave them to us because she knows how much you like them."

"I love Aunt Annie even more than peaches," Emma said sweetly. "I love you and Uncle Josh and Sophia most."

"We love you too Emma," Olivia kissed her head as she served her some spaghetti from the big container. "Ooh, we have garlic bread too." She handed a slice to each of the girls, before sitting down to serve herself and pass the bread to Josh. "You even ordered salad," she exclaimed, smiling at Josh. "What a great meal for such a long day. You have no idea how happy I am not to have to cook tonight."

"Yes I do. I felt exactly the same enthusiasm for the idea of cooking tonight as you did." Josh laughed.

"Emma, do you remember what your favorite thing your mom used to cook was?" Olivia asked, hoping to catch Emma's mind off guard and help her remember something from her forgotten past.

"No, but Stephanie cooked grilled cheese real good. I like grilled cheese." Emma answered.

"Who is Stephanie?" Olivia asked, her heart thumping overtime in excitement and shock that Emma seemed to be remembering something important.

"She took care of me after Mommy went away." Emma calmly took a bite of spaghetti.

"Where did your mommy go?" Olivia asked in a casual voice.

"Stephanie said she went to a rack to fight terrors," Emma stopped and her face was a study in puzzlement. "I don't remember my Mommy, but Stephanie said she's a sojer profapary. What's a sojer profapary, Aunt Livvie?" Olivia looked at Josh with her heart in her throat. Swallowing hastily, she answered Emma's question.

"A soldier is a person who is in the military and helps to keep people safe, kind of like a police officer. You know Uncle Josh used to be a police officer, right?"

"Yes, and Aunt Julie is a police Officer too. She keeps people safe too. My mommy keeps people safe? Where is she? Is she going to come back?"

"I'm not sure, honey. Do you remember what she looks like?"

"No. I just remember Stephanie said she's a sojer profapary." Emma answered, not seeming to be upset about not remembering her mother. "I forgot about that before, but I remember now."

"What do you remember about Stephanie?" Josh joined the conversation. "Do you remember her last name?"

"No, she's just Stephanie. She took care of me and made me food and everything." Emma frowned. "I liked Stephanie lots more than Darlene and Roberta, but I like you lots more than Stephanie. I love you and Aunt Livvie. I don't love Stephanie."

"We love you too, cupcake," Josh assured her, "You and Sophia too, more than anybody."

"I don't want to go live with Stephanie again. Can't I stay here with you still?"

"For right now, you sure can, Emma." Olivia smiled, forcing herself to remain calm and happy on the outside, even though she was worried sick on the inside.

As soon as dinner was over, and the kids were in bed, Josh and Olivia retired to the living room with Molly and Sheyna.

"Josh, Emma's mother must be in Iraq. I wonder why we haven't been able to find anything about Emma being missing?" Olivia sat sideways and cross legged on the couch facing Josh. "Wouldn't this Stephanie have reported her missing and wouldn't her mother have been back sometime during the last year or so?"

"Yeah, this whole thing with Emma is just really strange. From what she says, I am translating that to be that her last name is Parry or Perry or something like that and maybe she is a Private in some fighting branch of the military. Does that sound like what you heard?" Josh asked.

"Yes, it does. Thank goodness Emma is so articulate for her age and that she was able to remember that." Olivia sounded less than happy. "Oh Josh, how are we going to give her up?"

He pulled her against him and held her as her tears started. "I don't know, Liv. Let's see what we find. I'm very concerned that I haven't been able to find anything on her being missing. Who is this Stephanie, and if she really is her caretaker while her mom is in Iraq, why hasn't she reported her missing?"

"Maybe Emma isn't her real first name and we aren't really sure of her age either, you know. What if she's really four or six and her name is something entirely different?" Olivia got up and blew her nose. "Were there any missing kids that were close to her age that sounded at all like her?"

"Yes, but we managed to rule them out. Bob O'Brian has been helping me in his spare time as well, you know. He has better access to information, since he's still working at the State Police Headquarters. That's one of the things I miss about being on the job sometimes," Josh grimaced. "I'm lucky to have some good friends who still are though."

"Yes, and we have Julie too. The Birchwood Police Department may not have the prestige that the State Police has, but they're pretty awesome anyway."

"They definitely are," Josh agreed with a grin. "All former rivalries aside, we have a great police force here, local and state both, but even with their help and all their resources, we haven't been able to find anything on Emma."

"Until now," Olivia said in a small voice, "Now we need to look at Military records to see if we can find a female Private with a name like Perry. Then we'll have to turn Emma over to her mother or this Stephanie person."

"Maybe," Josh said gently, "But we don't know for sure if what she said is what we think. We'll worry about turning her over if and when we find her family. Let's see what happens before we scare ourselves."

Olivia sighed as Josh stood to hold her in a comforting embrace. "She is such an important part of our family already. I think Sophia would miss her as much as we would."

"You're probably right, but I'm still hoping it won't come to that. Maybe her mother isn't in the military at all. Profapary could mean something else entirely."

"Sojer sounds way too much like soldier though, so my hopes are a bit lower than yours." Olivia said sadly.

"I'm sorry, sweetheart. I want her to be our daughter too, but we can't get too freaked out until we know we have a reason to, right?" Josh gave her a wistful smile. "Where's that strength I know you have?"

"It's being beaten to a pulp by fear right now," Olivia smiled back, teary-eyed. "Don't worry, Josh, I won't fall apart. I'm just really worried."

He hugged her tight, "I know, Livvie. I am too, but we have to find out the truth if we can."

"I know, and we'll deal with whatever it is when we find it." Olivia stepped back and squared her shoulders. "We'll get through it together."

Josh smiled at her, "There's that courage you're so well known for." He hugged her and stepped back, "I hate to leave you when you're feeling so down, but it's getting late and I know Sophia will be up early, so you need your sleep."

"You're right on that one," Olivia cracked a weak smile. "She and Emma both will be up and ready for breakfast, not to mention Molly and Sheyna. I'm okay, sweetheart."

The front door opened behind them and Julie walked in, looking startled to see them right beside the door.

"Yikes," she laughed, "I almost ran you guys over. Are you coming or going, Josh?"

"I'm going, Julie," Josh laughed. "How did your friend's birthday party go?"

"It was nice. There were quite a few people there and a couple I'd never met, so I enjoyed it." Julie took off her heavy duty belt and headed toward her bedroom. "I'm sorry to take off on you, but I'm pooped and I'm going to hit the bed fast tonight."

"Sleep well," Josh and Olivia chimed as one, then laughed at their simultaneous replies, as Julie disappeared down the hall.

"You sleep well too, Liv. I'm sorry I have to go out of town right now, but I'll be back on Monday. If you need anything, call me. If you want to talk or rant or whatever, call me. The weekend is a bad time to try to talk to anyone in the military base offices anyway, so we'll work on it as soon as I get back." Josh kissed her and they clung together for a moment, sharing their worry as well as their strength.

CHAPTER SIX

Olivia's Saturday was filled with wedding preparations, as she met with Abby at Candlewick again to make sure the house was ready and to start the non floral decorations. Abby had hired a local florist to provide flowers, and she and Olivia were going to do some of the pre-decorating themselves. After all, Abby was an Interior Decorator and a very good one.

Annie spent the day at Olivia's house to babysit so it would be more convenient for everyone.

Olivia didn't want the kids to see the house until it was finished and they were ready to move in, so it would be a surprise. She was afraid to take Sheyna during the decorating phase in case she wanted to help decorate by hanging off all the ribbons and such, so she left her and Molly at home with Annie and the kids.

As soon as they were finished for the day, Olivia went into town to meet with the caterers. They'd asked her to stop by to taste the samples of the food she'd ordered for the reception to make sure everything was the way she wanted it. She happily informed them that the food was perfect after sampling all the delightful bits.

Since it was earlier than she'd expected to be done, she decided to see if she could find anyone who might remember the man, Thomas Jacobson, who'd been murdered fifty years ago in the house on Route 16 they were buying for their office.

According to what she'd found in the library, he had been a lawyer and was forty-four years old when he was killed. He'd apparently been shot at close range while sitting at his desk in the den.

Hmm, Olivia thought, *Either he knew the person who killed him well enough to let them into his house, or they were exceptionally good at breaking in quietly. I wonder if the murderer was connected to one of his cases.*

She drove to the most popular beauty shop to see if there was anyone around who remembered Thomas Jacobson from back in the day. He'd lived alone, and was unmarried, but as a single lawyer, and a fairly attractive man, judging from the grainy old photos on the microfilm, he might have been considered gossip worthy.

Although she found a few older ladies having their hair permed or colored, she wasn't successful at obtaining any information on the murdered man. One woman did tell her that she vaguely remembered Jacobson and that he'd been murdered, but the others had been too young to remember the murder at all.

Olivia had better luck at Spots, the small gas station /convenience store closer to her house. It was a gathering place for a lot of locals, including some of the older crowd, where they were free to sit at the tables on one side of the store and read the local paper or catch the latest gossip while having a cup of coffee and a homemade sandwich.

"Ayuh, I remembah the murdah," Mr. Davis confirmed. "The dead man was a lawyah who defended murderahs and othah bad criminals. My daddy always said, if you lie down with dogs, you can expect to get flea bites, so I guess it shouldn't have been a big surprise he was murdahed. It was still a bad business though."

Olivia cringed at the dogs and fleas reference, but had to acknowledge the unfortunate validity of it in many instances.

"Mr. Harris, did you ever have any thoughts as to who killed Thomas Jacobson?"

"I reckoned it had to be one of those criminals he was defendin'. As I recall, he was defendin' a man who'd murdahed his wife at the time. They never knew for suah, but I thought it was him who killed the lawyah," the garrulous elderly man replied in his old New England accent.

"Are you talking about Thomas Jacobson, who was killed fifty years ago or more in his own house?" Another older man joined in the conversation from the next table. "He was shot by some outraged husband, I'd say."

"An outraged husband?" Olivia inquired. "Why would you say that, Jack? Was he a philanderer?"

"Oh, he was a real skirt chaser, and he didn't care whether the woman was married with a family or not. He wasn't much better than those murderers and such he was defending if you ask me," Jack spat disgustedly as he got up and left the store, nodding brusquely to Olivia and Mr. Harris.

"Ayuh, I guess that rumah was true then," Mr. Harris shook his head. "I'd heard Jack's wife was seen riding in a car with Jacobson, but I nevah knew it if was true. She passed bout five yeahs ago, so I guess it doesn't mattah anymoah, except maybe to Jack."

"Do you think Jack could have killed him?" Olivia asked, watching Mr. Harris's face carefully.

He blew out a thoughtful breath. "I wouldn't have thought so, no, but I can't say he couldn't have done it eithah. You nevah know what can make a man snap."

Josh called while Olivia was putting the supper dishes in the dishwasher. He was still in Boston, helping his dad with some family business, and his dad came on the phone before they hung up.

"Olivia, I already asked Josh, but I wanted to ask you too. I have adopted a dog, and if you don't mind too much, I'd like to bring him with me. He's very well house trained and he loves everyone, people, dogs and cats. If it's a problem, I can leave him with my neighbor, but we're still bonding, so I'd rather not leave him."

"Peter, please bring him," Olivia insisted. "You know how much I love animals, and as long as he gets along with everyone, it won't be any problem at all. I can't wait to see you and to meet your new furry housemate."

~~~

Monday morning was beautiful with a gentle breeze and moderate temperatures. Josh called early to say he was home and to ask if Olivia wanted to head to the ski slopes with Emma and Sophia. He would meet them there, since he had to finish some paperwork his dad had sent home with him.

They hadn't managed to get to the slopes as planned over the weekend, since Josh had to leave to help his dad with something, so Olivia was eager to get the kids back on skis before they lost the muscle memory they were developing.

She got everyone fed and herself and the kids dressed in warm ski clothes. After promising Molly and Sheyna a nice romp later, she loaded Emma and Sophia into the SUV and headed to meet Josh.

The ski resort wasn't terribly busy on that Monday morning and they got their boots on quickly, leaving their shoes in cubbies in the lodge.

Emma was already pretty good at walking in the heavy ski boots, but little Sophia still had a hard time, as they were pretty heavy and awkward for her short little legs. Josh carried her so she wouldn't get tired out from walking as they walked to the little hill that had a Magic Carpet surface lift from the bottom to the top.

They all put on their skis, with Josh putting Sophia's on for her and Olivia holding Emma's hand as she stepped into her own.

They walked in their skis to the magic carpet which was like a flat rubber mat that moved much like an escalator, except without stairs. Olivia stepped onto the magic carpet in her skis, while Josh picked Sophia up and stood her on her skis in front of Olivia, then stepped onto the lift in front of Sophia so they could help her off at the top. Emma brought up the rear, proudly getting on the lift all by herself.

At the top, Josh hopped off and quickly turned around to take Sophia's hands and help her step off. He towed her to the side to wait for Olivia and Emma, who slid over to them as soon as they reached the top.

Josh skied backward in front of Sophia after they got her positioned properly in a narrow snowplow position. The hill was pretty flat so she slid slowly down, managing to follow Josh as he turned slightly. She seemed to instinctively figure out how to turn by just watching him. Her feet went where her head and eyes went.

They did the same run the same way again, but the

second time, Sophia managed to get herself off at the top, refusing to take Josh's hand for help. She was so proud of herself that she jumped up and down and fell over.

Olivia picked her up and they all praised her accomplishment. She giggled and grinned proudly, turning her skis toward the bottom and starting down without waiting for Josh to go first.

Olivia hurried past Sophia just in case she needed help, but the toddler made it down just fine.

After a few more perfect runs for Sophia, they decided to let her go into the daycare area and play with the other kids her age. They registered her and paid, then as she started playing easily without getting upset over the prospect of their leaving, they took Emma to the slightly larger and slightly steeper learning hill.

She'd already mastered getting on the slow chair lift with them the last times they'd gone skiing, so they hopped on and rode to the top with no further ado.

Emma did really well, maintaining her snowplow and controlling her speed and turns. She followed Olivia, as Josh brought up the rear.

After they'd done the short run a few times, one of Olivia's friends, who taught at the resort stopped them at the bottom by the lift. She said she was just starting a group clinic with some kids around Emma's age and ability level, and offered to let Emma join the group so she could ski with the other kids.

Emma was excited and begged to be allowed to join the group. Olivia and Josh thought it was a great idea and happily agreed. They arranged to meet Emma and her group in an hour and skated on their skis to one of the chair lifts that went to the summit of the mountains where they could find more challenging terrain.

On the ride up, Olivia told Josh what she'd heard about the murder from the two older men at the store.

"Even Mr. Harris didn't seem completely sure that Jack Stewart hadn't snapped and killed Jacobson," Olivia said with a grimace. "I always liked Jack, but I have to admit I really don't know him well at all . . . just to say hello and discuss the weather."

"Yeah, that's about how well I know him too. You know who does know him well though, is Martha Hodges over at the library. She and his wife, Ethel, were best friends, so I'd bet she'll know more than most."

"I'll stop by on the way home and see if she's there." Olivia lifted her ski tips and held her poles in one hand as they reached the top.

Josh followed Olivia as she chose a single black diamond glade run with trees that weren't too close together for their first challenging run of the day.

~~~~

On the way home, Emma was still excited about skiing with the kids and regaled Olivia with tale after tale of each kid's skiing prowess until she fell asleep. Sophia slept from the minute her head touched the car seat until they arrived home.

Luckily, Olivia had thought to call ahead and see if Martha was at the library and discovered that she was off on Mondays, so it would have to be the following day for that interview.

The little girls both talked about skiing while they ate their dinner.

"I ki too," Sophia yelled proudly, waving her spoon and knocking over her sippy cup. "I ki, I ki."

Olivia chuckled and picked up Sophia's cup from the floor. "Yes you did ski, Sophia. You and Emma both skied really well."

"You skied good Sophia," Emma praised her sister. "I skied good too. It was fun skiing with my new friends."

"I'm glad you got to make some new friends, Emma," Olivia smiled. "It sounds like you had a good time with them."

"Yes, I had a very good time. Can I ski with them again?"

"If they are around, I'm sure you can. Do you know their names and where they live?"

"Cammy and Nina live in Ohido and I forget where Benny lives. Maura lives in Birchwood."

"Well, Maura lives close by for sure then, so hopefully we can get her phone number from Cissy, your instructor and make a ski date with her." Olivia offered diplomatically. "We'll have to see about the others, if Cissy knows how to reach them, okay? Ohio may be a little far away for them to visit too often."

"Okay." Emma paused, "Maybe Ohido isn't that far."

As soon as they were done eating, Olivia bundled the kids up again and put Sophia in her stroller so they could walk Molly and Sheyna. Sophia fell asleep again once they started walking but Emma prattled away about skiing, happily telling Molly and Sheyna all about it.

Olivia got the kids bathed and tucked in quickly, and both were asleep almost before their heads touched the pillows.

Olivia loaded the dishwasher, curled up on the couch with a book and a cup of tea and tried to focus on reading instead of worrying about Emma and her 'sojer' mother.

Molly and Sheyna hopped onto the couch to keep her company and she felt better after a few cuddles with her furry girls.

"Molly, Sheyna how come you can always cheer me up so well?" Olivia hugged them both. "What would I do without either of you?" She tossed a ball for Molly who ran to catch it and bring it back for her to throw again. Sheyna swatted the ball and tried to grab it in her mouth to run and hide it, but it was too big, so she pouted a little until Olivia tossed her catnip toy for her.

The three played until Olivia's eyes started to droop and she yawned so wide she brought tears to her eyes. After taking Molly out for a few minutes in the back yard, she headed upstairs with Sheyna stopping off in Emma's room to pounce on her bed and curl up next to the child's head, while Molly raced to share Olivia's bed for the night.

As Olivia climbed into bed, she smiled over the animals' willingness to switch who they slept with, seemingly in perfect tune with Emma's wishes. She snuggled against Molly as she drifted off to sleep.

CHAPTER SEVEN

The next morning Olivia met Annie at the door. She'd come to babysit so Olivia could go interview some people at the retirement home who she thought might be good sources of information on the old murder.

Molly, Sheyna and the children were all happy to see Annie again, and there was a lot of excitement going on as Olivia left, with both kids clamoring to share their skiing experience, and Molly chiming in with an occasional woof of sheer happiness.

Olivia grinned as she closed the door to the SUV and started the engine. *I'm really lucky to have so many wonderful people and animals in my life,* she thought, then she sobered and breathed a silent prayer, *Please don't let us lose Emma.*

As she walked into the retirement home, Olivia mentally kicked herself for not bringing Molly and Sheyna so they could pay an extra visit to their usual residents who appreciated animals. When life was normal, and she wasn't in the middle of wedding plans, Olivia usually brought them once a week. There were several residents who had been forced to rehome their pets when they moved in and they missed them dreadfully.

Olivia and her friend, Pam McAllister, who was the

director of the retirement center, had finally come up with the best solution they could, besides Molly's and Sheyna's visits. Olivia had founded a program where new residents' pets could be adopted by volunteers from the community who would then allow them to visit their pets once a week, and they had more volunteers who could drive the residents to their pets' new homes for the visits if the adopted families weren't able to do it.

There was nothing they could do about residents who'd already given up their pets before the program had been in place, and the visits from Molly and Sheyna and other Therapy animals was the best Olivia and Pam could think of to do for them.

Olivia greeted Pam and explained what she was working on. Pam laughed when she heard that Olivia was once again involved in a mystery.

"I'm surprised you didn't say anything when we had lunch the other day. Knowing you, you'll solve it too, even after fifty years with no new clues."

Olivia chuckled and asked her friend which of the residents she thought might remember the circumstances surrounding the murder.

Pam thought for a few moments then wrote her a short list of names.

A querulous male voice bade her enter as she knocked at the door of the first person on her list.

"Good morning Mr. Phillips," Olivia said in a calm voice, proceeding to introduce herself and explain why she was there.

"I know it's been a long time, but do you remember anything about the murder that might help me discover who the killer was?"

"Why are you dredging up a murder from fifty years ago? Aren't there enough new murders and such to keep you occupied young lady? And why is a young lady like you involved in what should be police business?"

Yikes, Olivia thought, *this is going to be loads of fun.*

"Well, I'm curious about the murder because my fiancé and I just bought the house where it took place and we want to know the history of the house." Olivia tried to placate the man.

"You didn't ask about history, young lady," the cantankerous old man snapped. "You asked if I knew who killed someone fifty years ago. That's not history. That's nosiness and it might even be dangerous."

Olivia was slightly taken aback by his vehemence. "I think it's pretty dangerous if there is a killer walking around free among us, don't you?" she asked gently. "I'm not looking into it purely because I'm nosy, though I guess I am, when it comes to unsolved murders."

"Well, there's danger that comes unbidden, and then there's danger you that go looking for, and I'd say you're trying pretty hard to find it when you stick your nose into places it has no business being." The old man sat back and glared at her. "Now take your overly inquisitive, busybody nose out of my room and keep it out."

Olivia turned and fled, as one of his shoes came flying across the room, barely missing her head.

Wow, so much for that, she blew out a pent up breath. *I never expected anyone living here to act like that over my questioning them. He can't possibly be the murderer, can he?*

She paused in the hallway, her thoughts racing. *Why not? Whoever the murderer is, he would have to be at least in his mid sixties, if he was a teenager at the time, and probably quite a bit older, since he most likely had been an adult. I never stopped to think that the killer could easily be one of the home's residents. It's sad how we tend to think of them as just old people, forgetting that they had whole other lives before they ended up in here. Any one of them could have been a killer or a saint.*

The door to the next room on her list was open and the lady inside could be seen sitting in an armchair reading a book, so Olivia tapped lightly on the door, calling out to the woman as she did so.

"Olivia, what are you doing here without Molly and Sheyna?" the petite older woman asked in a cheerful voice. "It's not visitation day, is it?"

"Hi, Mrs. Martin," Olivia greeted her with a smile and a hug. "No, it's not visitation day, I'm afraid. I'm actually here to try to get information about a very old murder case that was never solved."

"Ooh, a mystery, and an old one at that," Mrs. Martin's face crinkled in a conspiratorial smile. "I've always loved mysteries."

"Me too," Olivia grinned, then immediately grimaced. "I wish all the residents felt that way."

"Why, who's been giving you a hard time?" she asked, putting her book aside.

"Mr. Phillips threw a shoe at me," Olivia said, caught between a cringe and a chuckle at her hasty retreat.

"Oh my! Well, he can be a curmudgeon, but he doesn't usually throw things at people. I wonder what on earth got into him?" she looked thoughtful.

"Was he ever in any trouble with the law that he might have had dealings with a defense attorney?" Olivia asked hesitantly. "The murder I was inquiring about was of a man named Thomas Jacobson, from fifty years."

"I remember that well," Mrs. Martin's eyes grew misty with memories. "The whole town was shaken to its core. Half the young women were hoping he'd look their way more than once, but he remained a steadfast bachelor."

"Did you ever hear any rumors of him being a philanderer?"

"There were rumors, definitely, and I'm sure a few of them were true. I wasn't one to spread gossip back then. Though now that I'm old, there isn't much else to do, so I do indulge a bit more, as long as it isn't the hurtful sort." She chuckled sheepishly. "As far as Charles Phillips having been in trouble with the law, I never heard of anything like that. He was a very straight laced sort of man and I seriously doubt he would have been up to anything illegal."

"What about his wife? Were there any rumors you recall about her and Thomas Jacobson?" Olivia grasped at straws.

"Not that I heard, no. Lenore Phillips was well matched with her husband back then, in being very upright and slightly holier-than-thou, so the idea of her having an affair with Thomas Jacobson is more than I can swallow."

"Maybe I just caught him at a bad time and it had nothing to do with the murder," Olivia smiled ruefully. "I think I'm steering clear of him for a while though, just in case."

Mrs. Martin chuckled, "If he's throwing shoes, I think I will too."

"So, if you don't mind telling me, who *did* you hear rumors about regarding having an affair with Thomas Jacobson?"

"There were a couple of married ladies I'd heard rumors about, besides the single ones. One was Rhonda Webber, who used to be married to Andy Webber before she divorced him and moved away." Mrs. Martin smirked slightly, "I believed that rumor easily. Rhonda always had an eye for a good looking man."

"Did Andy Webber seem unduly upset over the rumors?"

"He sure did. He threatened to kill Jacobson if he ever caught him sniffing around his wife," she chuckled as she reminisced. "He had an iron clad alibi though, since it turned out he was sleeping one off at the county jail when Jacobson was killed."

Olivia's face fell. "Well, that lets him out then. Who was the other married woman there were rumors about?"

"Ethel Stewart, Jack Stewart's late wife." Mrs. Martin frowned, "I was never sure what to think about that. Ethel wasn't a flighty type. She really didn't seem the sort to have an illicit affair, but Thomas Jacobson was a smooth talker and an extremely handsome man. Stronger women than Ethel Stewart have fallen for men like that."

"Do you think Jack Stewart would have been capable of killing Jacobson if he'd thought he was having an affair with his wife?"

"I think anyone is capable of committing murder under the right circumstances," Mrs. Martin replied shrewdly. "Jack was always a bit of a hot head, and yes, he was well known for his jealous streak where Ethel was concerned, even though I was never convinced he had reason, even with the rumors. It's a small town; there will always be rumors."

"Thanks so much for telling me all this," Olivia smiled

warmly at her friend. "Is there anyone else you can think of that might have had a reason to want Thomas Jacobson dead? What about other women? Did he have any relationships that went badly, which the woman may have killed him over?"

"Honestly, I can't think of anything like that. He wasn't the kind of man to get involved with any woman for long. Like I said before, he was a resolute bachelor." She thought for a moment, "There was a young girl who was terribly upset when he stopped seeing her after several dates." She paused, and spoke rather sadly, "I can't believe she would have killed him though. I could more easily picture her killing herself over him, than the other way around."

"What was her name?" Olivia asked gently, seeing her friend's distress.

"Gail Samuels," Mrs. Martin sighed. "She was my friend's little sister, a sweet girl, a couple of years younger than me, so she must have been around nineteen or twenty at the time of the murder. I think Jacobson was the first man she'd ever even had a crush on, and she fell hard for him. He was, of course, much older than her. Back then, it wasn't uncommon for young girls to have crushes on older, handsome men."

"It is still rather common, I think," Olivia smiled, "Though it is probably not the best idea for a marriage, then or now."

"You're quite right," Mrs. Martin replied, "For many reasons. My late husband, Don, was considerably older than me, and I was devastated when he died fourteen years ago. Our marriage was a good one. We loved each other dearly, but the age difference caused a lot of problems in our earlier years together, and it ultimately caused me to have to live all these years without him." She shook the sadness from her head.

"Anyway, getting back to Gail, I know how hard it hit her when he broke things off with her, but I can't consider for a minute that she would have killed him, even though I really do believe everyone is capable of murder. I could see her killing someone to protect another person, but not killing Thomas Jacobson because he'd broken her heart."

"There's no one else you can think of that might have had a motive?" Olivia asked after a moment of silence, "Anyone who'd possibly been a client of his?"

Mrs. Martin shook her head, "I'm sorry, Olivia, but I can't think of anyone else. If I do, I'll give you a call."

"Thank you so much. You've been a great help." Olivia gave her another hug, "I feel like I've gotten to know a lot more about the murder victim, as well as some of the people surrounding him."

"I've enjoyed our talk. Reading mystery books, like this one," she gestured to the Kathi Daley cozy mystery book on her nightstand, "is one of my favorite things to do. I enjoy them immensely, but getting to help in solving a real murder is something I don't often get to do, so thank *you* for the privilege."

"I'll let you know what I find out as I go along then," Olivia beamed. "You know so much about the people and the times surrounding the murder, that discussing it with you will be a huge help in solving it."

"What fun, this will be," the elderly lady chimed. "I will be Jane Marple and you can be Zoe Donovan, and we'll have it solved before you know it."

Olivia laughed, "You know we will . . . those are the

perfect identities for us to assume."

Olivia smiled to herself as she went to find Pam, after the last of her interviews was complete. She hadn't gotten any new information from the other three people at the home, but her mind felt quite busy sorting through what she'd learned from Mrs. Martin, so felt it had been a pretty productive morning.

"Thanks for making me the list of who to see, Pam," Olivia greeted her friend, as she found her in her office. "I think Mrs. Martin helped me a lot. By the way, what is with Mr. Phillips? He threw a shoe at me."

"He what?" Pam's eyebrows rose in astonishment.

"He became very upset as soon as I told him why I was there, and told me I was a busybody and to get out of his room. Then he threw a shoe at me," Olivia smiled ruefully.

"Wow," Pam ran her fingers through her hair in astonishment, "I've seen him get obnoxious, and rude, but I have never heard of him getting violent like that. I'll have to go and check on him. We can't have residents throwing things at people."

"I'm sorry to bring bad news, and please don't get too upset over it. He may have had a reason for my line of questioning to rile him like that, but I don't know for sure." Olivia felt bad to cause trouble for Pam, or for Mr. Phillips, even though she did consider him a suspect after his bizarre behavior.

"No, don't worry. I need to know when something weird like that is going on. I won't bring up the murder, but I will see if I can discover what set him off, whether it was you questioning him, or something else."

"Thanks Pam," she said, glad her friend wasn't the type to shoot the messenger. "On another note, Julie, is ready to adopt a dog or cat, as soon as my wedding is over and the house is free of me, the kids and all my relatives, who are coming in two weeks from Ireland. Do you have any new residents coming in that need homes for their pets?"

"I have someone coming in a couple of weeks who has two female cats we need to find homes for . . . no dogs right now," Pam answered, looking through the folders on her desk. "Do you think Julie would be interested in adopting two cats? Their owner really wants them to get adopted together, since they are very bonded."

"I'll ask her tonight," Olivia promised, "And let you know right away."

"I'm so excited about your wedding, Liv. You'd think it was me getting married." Pam laughed, hugging her friend. "How is the house coming along?"

"Oh Pam, it's perfect." Olivia beamed happily, "Abby has done an absolutely awesome job with everything. She's really amazing. Wait 'til you see it."

"I'm dying to," Pam laughed. "It's going to be nice to see your Mam and Da too. I miss them. I spent so many nights at sleepovers at your house when we were kids, that they're family to me."

"They think of you and Abby as daughters too," Olivia laughed. "I know they're going to be wicked thrilled to see you guys. Oh—would it be okay for Mrs. Martin to come to the wedding, and could she possibly come with you, if she wants to attend?"

"Definitely," Pam grinned, "Mrs. Martin is one of the nicest people here. I'd love to bring her. Do you want me to ask her?"

"That would be great. I'll send her an official

invitation tomorrow in the mail, but if you could ask her in the meantime, so she has time to think about it, I'd appreciate it. I feel bad for having forgotten to invite her earlier. It's been so crazy trying to plan the wedding so quickly."

"Consider it done. I think she will be thrilled to be invited," she paused. "Liv, if I hear of anything that has any bearing on your murder investigation, including why Mr. Phillips attacked you with shoes, I'll call you." Pam assured her as Olivia turned to leave. "That was odd behavior, even for him."

"Thanks so much for all your help, Pam," Olivia stepped into the hallway, "See you at the wedding rehearsal, if not before."

"I'll be there with bells on," Pam promised with a chuckle.

CHAPTER EIGHT

Olivia's next stop was the library, where she hoped to speak with Martha Hodges, the late Ethel Stewart's best friend.

Fortunately Martha was in and available to speak with Olivia.

"I'm surprised that you'd be looking into such an old murder, to be honest," Martha commented with a puzzled expression. "I heard about you solving the old Hill murder, but that was only a decade old or so. You may have your work cut out for you just finding enough of us old people still around to answer your questions about something that happened fifty years ago."

"Yes, it is a long shot, trying to look into a case from so long ago, but I'm having pretty good luck with a few of the people I've interviewed so far," Olivia smiled. "I'm glad you're willing to talk to me about your friend Ethel and the murder as well."

"I'm happy to be of help, but I really am not sure what you're looking for." She chuckled wryly, "Oh yes, I heard all the rumors about Ethel and Thomas. The whole valley heard them, I'm sure, but there was no more truth to them than that bears can fly."

"So, you're saying the rumors were all false?"

"The ones about Ethel and Thomas were false for sure. Ethel detested the man. She went to him for a consultation on a private legal matter and someone saw her coming out of his office and the rumor started. It took on a life of its own really quickly, like most rumors do," Martha pursed her lips.

"Can you tell me what she spoke with him about?"

"I promised her I wouldn't tell anyone, but I guess it wouldn't matter, now that she's passed on. I certainly don't feel any such allegiance to Jack, being the whole thing was his fault," Martha sighed. "She found out that Jack had been losing their money on several ridiculous 'get rich quick' scams that a friend of his had talked him into investing in, and she thought a lawyer might be able to help to get the money back, as they really could ill afford to lose it."

"I thought Jacobson was a criminal lawyer," Olivia was puzzled.

"He was, but poor Ethel didn't pay attention to things like that, so she never realized there was a difference, until she went to see him. He was so condescending to her about it." Martha shook her head, "I wish she'd mentioned it to me before she went to see him, but she never said a word until the rumors started flying and I asked her what was going on. She was so embarrassed and upset that people could think she'd do that. She was in tears over it, and Ethel wasn't the type to cry, at least not in front of anyone."

"That's such a shame. Rumors are very hurtful, but people don't seem to realize it," Olivia said sadly. "Did she get over her embarrassment once the novelty wore off and people stopped talking?"

"Yes, thankfully, she did. Thomas was killed a couple

of months afterward and people's talk quickly turned to the murder and forgot all about the affair rumors." Martha smiled, as if satisfied that her friend had finally gotten some peace from the gossipmongers.

"Speaking of the murder, what was the rumor mill coming up with on that?"

"There were a lot of different rumors going and just as many crazy theories," Martha chuckled. "Most people were saying it had to be one of his clients that had gotten more time than he'd expected to get and blamed him for it."

"Did you hear any names being bandied about?"

"As far as the criminals, not really, though I seem to remember he'd had one client who'd just gotten out of jail recently and they were saying that he'd threatened him during the sentencing years ago. I can't remember his name off hand ... Darwin, Darby ... something like that."

Olivia wrote the names down along with the other notes she'd been taking.

"What about other people, besides the clients?"

"Well, Ethel's husband, Jack was one, along with Andy Webber, but he was ruled out pretty soon, since he was in jail at the time. I can't really think of anyone else right now."

"Did you have any suspects, yourself?"

"No. I knew Jack hadn't done it. He wouldn't have had the gumption. He was good at blustering and making Ethel feel guilty, even though she knew she hadn't done anything wrong, but he'd never have shot someone in cold blood." She thought for a second, "Actually, I could see him shooting Thomas if he'd caught them together in a compromising position, but since they were never together in that way, it's impossible. He did dislike the man after the rumors started, but I just can't see him having the nerve unless it was in a moment of intense anger and he couldn't control himself. He just wasn't cold enough for that type of murder."

"An interesting choice of words," Olivia murmured. "So you feel that the murder was planned and committed by a cold individual?"

"Yes." Martha replied. "The police found no signs of anyone breaking in, and Thomas's gun was present and accounted for, so whoever killed him, must have been someone he knew and felt comfortable enough with to allow in his house at night."

"And the killer brought a gun, so he most likely planned to use it," Olivia finished up the account, nodding her head. "Yes, it does sound like a more calculating murderer than Jack would have been, the way you described him."

"I doubt Thomas would have admitted Jack Stewart to his home, especially at night. Jack had made no secret of his dislike of the man, though, unlike Andy Webber, he had never publicly threatened him." Martha stood, apparently signaling her desire to end the conversation.

"Thank you so much for your time, Martha." Olivia rose as well, and folded her notebook, placing it in her purse. "Please give me a call if you happen to think of anything else that might help me figure out who killed Thomas Jacobson."

It was lunchtime by the time Olivia left the library and her stomach rumbled, so she stopped to pick up a sandwich from the deli.

As she started to push the door open, she felt a rush of wind on her cheek; there was a huge crashing sound, and the Deli's glass door shattered into a million pieces in front of her.

Olivia screamed, dropping her hand from the door handle and running inside, crunching glass under her feet as she dove through the little swinging half door to hide behind the counter.

Two frightened employees crouched with her, as someone in the back screamed.

Olivia dialed 911 on her cell phone and reported what had happened, then cautiously peeked around the little swinging door to see if there was anyone there, and spotted a paper wrapped brick lying amidst the glittering shards of glass. People were starting to form a crowd outside, and Olivia realized that whoever had thrown the brick was most likely long gone.

She stood and walked to the entrance, carefully stepping through the glass, avoiding the brick.

"Please, if you could all step away from the entrance, so you don't get injured, but if you saw anything at all, please remain nearby until the police arrive so you can tell them." Olivia was learning the drill for incidents like this, having managed to be in the middle of a few already.

Several people walked away, but three remained, moving back slightly, but obviously planning to wait for the police.

Olivia's cell phone rang, as the first police cars screeched to a stop in front of the deli.

It was Josh. He'd heard from Julie, who'd heard the call come in and called him right away, while the dispatcher was sending people out to the scene.

Olivia assured him that she was fine. Luckily for her, the brick had missed her and the glass had all been sent inward by the impact. One of the deli employees had a small laceration on his cheek, but there had been no serious injuries.

Olivia could feel Josh's nerves still twanging as she ended the call to speak with the officers.

Her thoughts were in chaos as she tried to figure out why the brick had been thrown. *Was it connected to the old murder? Am I making someone nervous? If it wasn't connected, it was an awfully big coincidence.*

She went over everything that had happened with the Birchwood Police Officers, who then also interviewed the three witnesses, and the deli employees.

From what Olivia was able to gather, listening to the other interviews, the only thing anyone had really seen was a light green car driving away rather quickly, though one of the witnesses swore it was a light blue car.

Josh pulled up and parked half a block down the street in an empty spot, and walked briskly to where she stood outside the shattered door.

He looked around intently, taking in everything, including Olivia, then silently took her into his arms.

Olivia held him as tightly as he did her, feeling his tension from her close call finally start to ebb.

He squeezed her hand gently and moved to speak with one of the police officers, leaving her for a moment, as he knew he'd get more information alone.

Olivia watched curiously, as the other cops took pictures and then collected the brick from the debris after taping off the area in front of the deli to keep people from wandering in and getting cut or messing up their crime scene before they were done.

Josh returned and they walked toward Olivia's car,

where they could speak freely.

"So, did he tell you anything more than I already know from being there?" Olivia asked impishly.

Josh grinned and rolled his eyes, "You're going to give me a heart attack one day, Liv. You always manage to be where the action is."

"Not by choice, Josh," Olivia chuckled. "Trust me, I just wanted to buy a sandwich."

They climbed into her car where it was warmer and they couldn't be overheard.

"No one saw anyone, only a car, and they can't agree on the color or make of it. They're not even sure it was involved in the crime. Someone could have run from the alley and thrown the brick and run back in without being seen at all." Josh shook his head, "Not much help from the witnesses.

"There was a paper wrapped around the brick, as you may have noticed," Josh continued. "It had a poem of sorts written on it. *"Little Miss Nosy thinks she's a cop, what will it take to make her stop?"*"

"Oh my . . . how lovely," Olivia grimaced. "I have a literary stalker. I've heard of poetic justice, but poetic brick throwing is a new one."

Josh sighed heavily, "Here we go again. That had to have been for you. Either the con artist thinks we're getting close, or the murderer from fifty years ago is alive and not happy that you're looking into it after all these years."

"I think it must be related to the old murder case, Josh." Olivia frowned, "Nothing else makes sense."

"Unfortunately, I think you may be right." Josh ran his fingers through his wavy dark hair in vexation, "Which means I'm going to have to start worrying about you again.

I've barely recovered from the worry of the last time we were involved in a murder investigation."

"Well, that runs both ways, as we've discussed before." Olivia reminded him gently. "If someone thinks we're on to something they don't want us to find out, they will be just as likely to go after you, as me."

"Yes, I know, Livvie, but I can't help it if it scares me more when they go after you." He sighed heavily, "You did everything right, just like your training taught you, and I am very proud of you. I won't chide you too much for not wearing your gun, as it wouldn't have helped in this case, but I really want us to get to the range more often. You're a good shot, but until you feel confident enough that you'll carry your gun, that won't do any good."

"Okay, I'll train whenever you want, and I'll carry it once I feel sure of my ability not to accidently shoot someone." Olivia grimaced slightly, "It just feels so awkward to carry, and I'm afraid of it going off when I draw it, and shooting an innocent bystander or something."

"You'll stop feeling that way once you grow more confident, and that only comes through training." Josh smiled, rubbing her hand. "As a PI, you really should be carrying."

"Oh, by the way, speaking of guns and such, Julie said she is going to be working the night shift the next couple of weeks, so if we pick up food, we should count her out." Olivia informed him. "She also said she was very interested in the two cats Pam told me about, that will be needing homes, so that is one piece of good news on this crazy day."

A sharp tap on Josh's window startled them both.

Josh opened his door, looking a bit exasperated, as the

guy who'd knocked, one of the tourists milling around, asked him if he'd seen what had happened.

He controlled his temper, and merely told the man that it wasn't a good idea to knock on people's car windows, as someone might get upset and punch him.

Olivia just shook her head, amazed at the man's obnoxious behavior.

Josh walked around to her side of the car, and as she lowered the window, he leaned in and kissed her.

"I want to take you out for dinner tonight. I'll order some food for Annie and the kids, if she is up for extending her babysitting until we get home." Josh gave her a sexy smile, "I won't have you to myself for a long time now, since your folks are arriving soon and the next three weeks are going to be even more crazy than usual."

Olivia agreed that it was a good idea, knowing how hectic her house was already, without her parents and grandparents being there.

"I'll run home and make sure Annie is up for it, spend a few minutes with Emma and Sophia and take Molly and Sheyna to the park for a quick romp, then I can take a shower and get dressed." Olivia thought quickly.

"Wow, I got tired just listening," Josh laughed. "We'll go somewhere nice and relaxing, to make up for all the rushing around I'm causing you."

"I don't mind rushing around, but yeah, some place relaxing sounds good."

They kissed again, and Olivia raised the window as Josh walked back toward his car.

Olivia noticed the deli owners helping their employees to cover the broken door with boards. She guessed that the police department would be keeping an eye on it until they could get the glass replaced tomorrow.

She hadn't wanted to let Josh know that she felt a tiny bit shaken from her experience still, but she could feel her hands trembling slightly now that the adrenaline rush had dissipated. She took a deep breath to steady herself and headed home.

Annie was delighted to be asked to stay longer, even offering to spend the night. Olivia agreed that would be a great idea, though she'd be back before too late, as there weren't many places open super late in town. She didn't want Annie to have to drive home late, so she made up the guest room for her.

Emma and Sophia were happy to see her and Emma told her all about their day, while Sophia chimed in, frequently babbling in baby talk, but occasionally speaking in small sentences too. They were both excited about Annie spending the night, though a little less so once they realized that meant Olivia was going out.

Annie nixed the idea of ordering food for their dinner, and happily busied herself in the kitchen, cooking for the kids and herself.

Olivia grabbed Molly's and Sheyna's harnesses and leads and they both excitedly pranced around her while she got them ready for their walk.

The short drive to the park was uneventful and Molly had loads of fun once they arrived. She ran back and forth across the park, returning to dance around Olivia and Sheyna.

Sheyna was much more dignified, walking sedately beside Olivia, for the most part, but finally giving in to the urge to pounce on a piece of paper that was blowing on the ground in front of her.

Olivia retrieved the paper and put it in her pocket to throw away later.

She took the girls home and fed them, then hopped into the shower and dressed quickly, finishing with a light touch of makeup, just as Josh arrived to pick her up.

As they'd agreed earlier, he waited in the car, while she kissed the children, hugged Molly and Sheyna and said a quick, thankful goodbye to Annie. If he'd come in, it would have been an hour before they'd have been able to extricate themselves from everyone and get on their way, since the kids would have been so eager to tell him everything they'd already told Olivia.

Josh held her hand for a moment as he backed the car into the road, "How are you feeling? I know you had to have been more upset by that whole thing than you let on."

"Yeah, I was a little shaken up, but I feel fine now. Seeing the kids and the time with Molly and Sheyna calmed me down." Olivia assured him. "It really is possible that it was a coincidence, even though it may not be likely."

"Yes, anything is possible," Josh agreed with a snort. "It's even possible that we could solve one murder without you being in danger, but I'll believe it when I see it."

Olivia laughed, "Well, one can dream, right?"

"Yep, that's probably as close as we'll get to it happening too," Josh grinned wryly. "On another topic, I found someone who'd seen our scammer today, but he'd introduced himself as Mark, not Roger. She didn't fall for his scam, and told him off in no uncertain terms."

"Good for her," Olivia cheered. "Though, I guess that leaves us back where we started from, unless she gave you a new clue about him."

"Unfortunately, no," Josh said resignedly. "She just

sent him off with a flea in his ear as my mom used to say."

"Well, at least he didn't get anything from her."

"There is that," Josh grinned. "Hopefully, the next person he tries to con will pick up some good clues before she or he sends him off."

Dinner at the lovely Swiss restaurant was both relaxing and romantic. As always, the food was exquisite.

Olivia felt the tension of the day ebb away, as she gazed into her fiancé's warm eyes over the light of the small candle.

"We should get away more often," Josh smiled. "As much as I love being with Emma and Sophia, and having family dinners at your house with all of us together, I also love getting to spend a little romantic alone time like this, with just the two of us once in a while."

"You're right," Olivia agreed, "We haven't gone out alone like this but a couple of times in the past two months. I hadn't realized it, but I've missed it too."

"Well, it's going to be a hectic time until the wedding, but we'll have our honeymoon to relax and enjoy each other's company," Josh said wagging his eyebrows in a comically suggestive way.

Olivia laughed, blushing slightly as she did so, "Yes, I'm sure we can more than make up for the lack of alone time then."

Josh laughed, winking, as he poured her some wine.

Once Josh had taken her home and left, Olivia went upstairs and kissed the sleeping children goodnight, then, as Annie was already in bed, she made a cup of tea and sat down on the couch with her notebook and a pencil.

She decided to make a list of suspects in the murder. She wrote them in order of how she remembered them:

Jack Stewart; Mr. Phillips; the as yet unknown man Jacobson had defended for killing his wife; Rhonda Webber; the client of Jacobson's who threatened him, Darby or Darwin, or something similar, if Martha Hodges had the name right.

She couldn't think of anyone else, so she put the notebook away and finished her tea thoughtfully before heading to bed.

CHAPTER NINE

The first thing Olivia thought of when she awoke was how grateful she was that she'd been alone at the deli the previous day. She would never have forgiven herself if one of her loved ones had gotten hurt because she was investigating something, especially something she hadn't even been hired to investigate.

Whoever had thrown the brick obviously didn't mind the thought of hurting me and probably wouldn't have minded hurting Josh either. They may not have even cared if I'd had Molly and Sheyna with me, but would they have still thrown it if I'd been carrying Sophia and holding Emma's hand? How ruthless is this person? Where do they draw the line? Olivia sighed as she got up.

Josh called to let her know he was doing some online research for the case they'd been hired to work, and would be in the office all morning. She promised to stop by with Molly and Sheyna later.

On the spur of the moment, Olivia decided to take Molly and Sheyna to visit at the retirement home, since Annie was staying with Emma and Sophia today.

She'd felt guilty for missing the last week's visitation and it would be a great opportunity for her to speak to Mrs. Martin again, just in case she'd thought of anything else. *I really shouldn't miss these visitations,* she thought to herself. *The residents miss their pets, and it does them so much good to have the girls visit.*

It had only been a day since she was there last, so it was unlikely Mrs. Martin would have anything more to tell her, but Olivia knew it would be good to have someone to talk with about the mystery, who'd actually known the people involved back then, plus she genuinely liked Mrs. Martin.

Pam was happy to see her and the girls, and delighted to hear that Julie was interested in the new resident's cats, though surprised she hadn't mentioned it at the dress fitting.

Olivia did her usual routine of taking the girls to visit all the people on their schedule. She thought about checking to see if Mr. Phillips might be more congenial this time, if she tried to question him, but decided to wait and see Mrs. Martin first, then check in with Pam in case she had any thoughts on it.

Molly and Sheyna both had a good time getting pets and hugs from 'their people' and Olivia was so glad she'd decided not to skip the visit again, vowing to be strict with herself about it, and not miss unless she really had to.

Mrs. Martin was happy to see her and excited about going to Olivia's wedding.

"I've always loved weddings," she smiled reminiscently. "It is such a beautiful occasion when two people want to dedicate their lives to each other. You and Joshua make a lovely couple too."

"Thanks Mrs. Martin. I'm so glad you're going to be able to come."

"So am I," The old woman smiled brightly. "I imagine you didn't invite Mr. Phillips," she asked, tongue in cheek.

Olivia laughed, "No, that seemed a little too dangerous. I'm fine with rice or confetti being thrown at me, but shoes are a bit much."

She sobered, "You know, someone threw a brick at me yesterday when I went to the deli for lunch in the afternoon. It had a threatening poem attached to it. The shoes made me think of it. Mr. Phillips couldn't have gone there, I suppose, right?"

Mrs. Martin frowned, "A poem? It seems highly unlikely he could have sneaked out and done that with no one knowing about it, though if I recall correctly, both he and Lenore were very much into poetry, so that part sounds like him. Did you ask Pam if he'd been missing at all yesterday?"

"Not yet," Olivia replied. "I know it's a long shot, but the retirement center is quite close to the deli, so it is possible, if he is mobile enough."

"He gets around pretty good for such an old codger," Mrs. Martin chuckled. "I saw him practically running down the hallway last week, when he saw Mrs. Foster headed his way. She has the hots for him, believe it or not. Of course she's had a thing for almost every man in the place at one time or another."

Olivia chuckled along with her, "Well, if he can move that fast, then he is staying on the suspect list for sure."

"I'd leave him there," Mrs. Martin agreed. "He does seem prone to throwing things when he's mad, so he's as likely a candidate as anyone I can think of, even though the brick sounds more violent that I'd have though him. You're right about it being close enough for him to slip over there and back if he timed it right. It's not like we're watched constantly or locked in. After all, it isn't really a prison … it just feels like one sometimes," She smiled rather sadly.

"I'm so sorry," Olivia said, giving her a hug. "I can imagine it must feel that way quite often."

"Oh, not so much to me," Mrs. Martin assured her, though Olivia could see that it did. "I was thinking of some of the other residents . . . even Mr. Phillips, grouchy bear that he is."

Sheyna moved to rub against Mrs. Martin's hand as she sensed the old lady's sadness. Mrs. Martin gratefully petted her, rubbing her between the ears with her thin, fragile looking hand.

"Some of the residents really don't have anyone at all, and the ones like Mr. Phillips, who already have a mad on at the world, can get awfully lonely at times," Mrs. Martin sighed. "He was looking particularly upset this morning when I saw him at breakfast."

"Do you think it was because of yesterday . . . maybe just from my questioning him?"

"It's possible, and it's possible that he threw the brick at you too, or that it had nothing to do with any of this." Mrs. Martin shook her head in frustration. "I wish I could tell you for sure, but I just don't know."

"Don't feel discouraged," Olivia smiled at her, sympathetically. "Everything you tell me is helping, even if it's just giving me a better picture of the people I'm asking about."

"Well, if I could give you a good picture, I'd be happy to, but with Charles and Lenore Phillips, it's even harder than with most. They were good people, happy and friendly . . . nothing like he is now; though he was always a bit of a hot-head, he certainly never threw things at people." She paused for a moment and a sad look came over her face. "Of course, once Matty died, neither of them was ever the same."

"Who was Matty?" Olivia asked gently.

"She was their daughter." Mrs. Martin smiled a sad smile. "She was a sweet girl, had a lot of friends and was quite popular in school. She was her parents' whole life. The drunk who hit her car and ran her off the road ruined more than her life that night."

"Oh no, no wonder he is so angry," Olivia's face filled with pain. "Was Jacobson the attorney for the drunk driver that killed Matty?"

"Come to think of it, yes, he was. The man who hit her car was fairly wealthy, and easily able to pay Thomas to represent him. The judge let him off with only six months in jail, and a big fine." Mrs. Martin sighed heavily, "Charles and Lenore were devastated and furious, as you can imagine."

"I'm not surprised they were," Olivia said in astonishment. "How could he get such a light sentence if he killed someone while he was driving drunk? How old was Matty when she died?"

"She'd have been around eighteen or nineteen, I guess. Charles is getting close to ninety now, and he and Lenore were quite young when they married."

"I feel so sorry for him, now. What an awful thing to go through. My questions must have brought it all back to him," Olivia said sadly. "Even if he had nothing to do with the murder, he'd have every right to be angry at me for putting him through all those emotions again."

"Well, throwing a shoe at you for it is one thing, but if he threw that brick at you, that's something else entirely," Mrs. Martin said wryly. "If he could do that, knowing it could seriously injure you or kill you, then it's not so hard for me to picture him killing Thomas Jacobson."

Olivia petted Molly thoughtfully, "I can more easily see him killing the lawyer in the heat of the moment, than I can sneaking out to look for me and trying to kill me because he was afraid I'd figure it out. So far, from all you've told me, and from what I've seen personally, he is a quick tempered man, who acts without thinking when angered, rather than the type to plan a cold-blooded murder."

"I think you may be right. Charles always was a bit hot-headed, but there's no way to tell what someone might do when their child has been killed," Mrs. Martin's expression was thoughtful. "Grief can do strange things to the mind."

"Actually, thinking about it, wouldn't he have had more reason to kill the judge than the lawyer, if he was upset over the verdict?" Olivia frowned, "I mean, the lawyer just did what he was hired to do, but the judge is the one who made the decision to just slap the guy on the wrist."

"That's a good point, my dear," Mrs. Martin brightened, and smiled at Olivia. "I'd really hate to think I'd been living just down the hall from a murderer for all this time and never knew it. He's been through a lot, with Matty being killed, then his wife dying a few years ago. I've always been sad for him, rather than afraid of him."

"I'm starting to feel that way too," Olivia sighed. "I just really don't see that he had either the right motive or temperament for that murder . . . if it had been the judge who was killed, maybe, but not Jacobson. I think we're back to square one."

"As much as I'd hate to think it was Charles Phillips, eliminating him is going to deplete our suspect pool significantly, isn't it?" Mrs. Martin grimaced. "Well, I'll keep wracking my brain to try and think of anyone else that might have had a motive, but right now, I am fresh out of ideas."

"Thanks, Mrs. Martin," Olivia smiled. "It really is helpful to talk with you about this. It's extremely difficult trying to look at something that happened so long ago, but even more so, because I don't really know many of the people who were around back then."

Mrs. Martin laughed, "Well, once in a while being older than dirt has its perks. I love being able to help you out. It's a nice break from the usual monotony this place has to offer." She scratched Sheyna's ears in a parting caress, and reached to pet Molly goodbye as well. "Thanks so much for bringing the girls and for your kindness in including me in your investigation."

"It's more of a kindness for you to help me than otherwise, Mrs. Martin," Olivia assured her with a hug. "I'd be completely at a loss without you on this."

Olivia, Molly and Sheyna went in search of Pam. They found her juggling several suitcases as a new resident was being introduced to the facility, and all her staff seemed to be busy elsewhere.

Olivia laughingly took charge of one of the cases, holding Sheyna in her other arm, as she followed Pam to the resident's room.

"Mr. Abe Turner, this is Olivia McKenna, and, Molly, her Golden Retriever and Sheyna, her cat. They are certified therapy animals and you are welcome to sign up for them to visit you, if you like animals. She tries to bring them one day a week." Pam and Olivia set the man's luggage down in his room as Pam introduced them.

"Pleased to meet you Miss McKenna," the elderly man said gallantly, offering his hand to shake.

"It's my pleasure, Mr. Turner," Olivia liked him instantly, as he petted Sheyna, then stooped to greet Molly, who lifted her paw daintily for a paw shake.

"Well, I just might enjoy it here after all, if we're going to have such charming visitors," he chuckled to Pam. "I had expected to be all on my own with a bunch of old fogies like myself, and nothing to do, but whine and moan about our no good relatives who'll never visit. This . . ." he nodded toward Olivia and the girls, ". . . This is a pleasant surprise."

"I hope you'll sign up for the visits, Mr. Turner," Olivia smiled. "The girls are obviously already smitten with you," she chuckled, as Sheyna head-butted his hand asking for more pets.

"The feeling is mutual, and you can be sure I will sign up immediately, just as soon as this young lady allows me near the signup sheet," he twinkled his eyes toward Pam.

"Then, I'll look forward to seeing you soon, Mr. Turner," Olivia beamed, as she led Molly back into the hallway so he could get settled in.

Pam joined her and they walked back toward Pam's office.

"He's such a nice man," Olivia commented. "The girls already adore him, after just a couple of minutes with him. Hmm, I wonder if he might know anything about the old murder."

"It's possible, I suppose," Pam said, "But I really don't know him well enough yet to say. We should give him a chance to get used to the place first, but you're welcome to speak with him about it next time you come."

"If I haven't gotten it solved by then, which unfortunately, I doubt I will have, then I'll definitely ask him," Olivia grinned. "If nothing else, he's really nice to talk to, so charming and gentlemanly. I thought Josh and his dad were about the only gentlemen left, besides my own Da and Pop."

"Well, if you happen to find another one, and he's semi-decent looking, roughly our age and straight, please send him my way," Pam retorted laughing. "I think you might have snagged the last one of those though, Liv."

"Speaking of gentlemen and non-gentlemen, have you noticed anything about Mr. Phillips?"

"No, and I didn't mention the shoe episode, since he was acting very subdued and a little depressed by the time I saw him," Pam lifted the corner of her mouth in a sad half-smile. "I didn't want to chastise him and make him feel even worse than he obviously felt."

"I don't blame you. After my talk with Mrs. Martin today, I'm seriously starting to doubt that he had anything to do with killing Jacobson all those years ago. He doesn't fit the bill, really." Olivia sighed, "I wish I could figure out who did fit it that easily."

"So, will you be bringing the girls right up until the wedding, or are you going to take a break from it?"

"I'm planning to keep bringing them, unless it becomes impossible. I think we'll manage. The residents miss them too much when we skip visits."

"They really do," Pam agreed. "It's the highlight of the week for many of them. They all love the girls' visits and I think some of them enjoy talking with you just as much as petting Molly and Sheyna. They don't get nearly enough visits from relatives and friends."

"Well, we'll be here until the wedding then, for sure. I'll be gone for two weeks after that for the honeymoon, but Molly and Sheyna and the kids will be staying with Annie." Olivia smirked, "Abby is going to be staying with her mom to help out, so you might be able to get her to bring the girls to do their visits while we're gone."

"Oh no, I will not be indebted to Abby. She'll have me schlepping antique furniture all over town in my van for the next month," Pam laughed, rolling her eyes.

Olivia laughed, "Nah, you can tell her it's a favor for me. I already owe her big, so one more won't matter."

"Speaking of that, I am so excited to see Candlewick House. Did it turn out as nice as you thought it was going to?"

"Even more stunning, Pam," Olivia beamed. "It's like a fairytale castle to me . . . beautiful, majestic, and yet very welcoming, all at the same time. Abby did an absolutely awesome job with it."

"She is really good at what she does, and she knows you so well, she can picture what you'd want."

"Exactly," Olivia agreed. "She got right in my head when she was decorating. I could barely believe my eyes when I saw it." She bent to gather up Molly's and Sheyna's leashes, and set Sheyna down so she could walk with them. "Well, we'd better run now. We'll be back next week or perhaps sooner, if I have half a chance."

The town was fairly quiet as Olivia drove to their rented office space. Josh's SUV was in the tiny parking lot shared with the business next door, but there was room for two more vehicles, so Olivia pulled in next to Josh, and unloaded the girls.

"How's the research going," Olivia asked, giving Josh a hug and kiss as they walked in to find him glued to the computer. "Anything new on the con man?"

"So far, a big lot of nothing on that," Josh frowned, "I was starting to wonder if the prints on the contract papers were even his, or if he'd worn gloves when handling them, so I called Elaine, and she sheepishly admitted that it had been chilly when they'd signed the papers and that yes, he'd probably been wearing gloves, though she hadn't really noticed one way or the other." He shook his head disgustedly, "When I asked her to think hard, she thought they'd both been wearing thin driving gloves . . . so the prints are likely from some copy person at an office supply store or something. I should have thought to ask her sooner."

"Oh, well, either way, the prints didn't show in the databases, so we aren't any worse off than before. Actually," she thought for a second, "We're better off, because if they were his prints, and not in the databases, it would be even harder to ever identify him. At least this way, if we get his real prints, we might get lucky right away."

"That's my Pollyanna," Josh laughed. "I love your optimism, Livvie. I tend to get myself into a dark blue funk over little setbacks sometimes, and I can always count on you to make me see the bright side."

Olivia hugged him, "Well, dark blue funks are no fun, so someone has to set you right."

He laughed as he sat back from the computer and invited Molly to jump up in his lap. Sheyna was already sitting on the desk, batting lightly at the mouse.

"I thought about stopping at the deli to bring us lunch, but couldn't quite bring myself to do it with the girls along, so I'm going to leave them with you and run across to the bakery for sandwiches."

"I don't blame you," Josh said soberly. "I'd be surprised if you didn't have misgivings about going to the deli for a while after an experience like that. I know I would."

"Well, I'll get over it as soon as we catch the culprit, but for now, I'm watching my surroundings as best I can, and avoiding the deli like the plague," she laughed. "Egg salad on rye with a Kosher dill sound good to you?"

"Sounds perfect," Josh laughed along with her. "I'm glad you're taking this seriously, and being careful. I worry, you know."

"I know, and I hope you're being careful too." Olivia said earnestly. "You know the door was unlocked when I arrived. We might consider keeping it locked when we're working on cases that seem dangerous."

"You're right, we should do that, and I should have thought of it myself," Josh hugged Molly, then eased her off his lap and stood. "I'll lock it behind you, and open it when you get here, so you don't have to fumble with the key while carrying the bags, or I can go and you stay if you'd rather," he added.

"No, I'll go," she smiled. "I'm still not sure if I want to grab some nice dessert for our dinner, so I'll take a peek at what they have made today." Josh locked the door behind her and went back to his frustrating research with a renewed optimism.

CHAPTER TEN

The bakery was empty except for the owner, and she wanted Olivia to taste a new frosting she'd come up with, to see if she'd be interested in having it on her wedding cake.

"Ooh, that's divine, Amy. Yes, I think it would be perfect. Do you mind giving me a tiny bit for Josh to try to make sure he agrees? What is it?"

Amy smiled broadly, happy with Olivia's enthusiasm for her new creation. "It's a mild lemon, orange cream cheese frosting. I made sure to keep the citrus flavors mild, so they wouldn't be overpowering."

"It's wonderful, and I am pretty sure Josh will love it too."

"Great. Let me know what he thinks. Now what can I get you for lunch?"

Olivia knocked at the office door, her hands laden with food bags and a small torte in a box for the night's dessert.

Josh opened the door and took the packages from her hands, while she locked the door behind her.

"Here, Josh, after your sandwich, you have to try the frosting Amy concocted for the wedding cake so I can let her know if we want it." Olivia handed him the little plate with white cake and the succulent frosting.

"Well, it looks good," Josh sniffed at it as he set it down to open his sandwich, "Smells good too, kind of lemony, but sweet."

"I think you'll like it." Olivia bit into her egg salad and Molly gave her a look from the floor.

"Yes, Molly, you and Sheyna will get a treat as soon as we're done," Olivia assured her, with a chuckle. "This sandwich is excellent." She set aside a small bite for Sheyna, and a slightly larger one for Molly.

"Have you had a chance to look into Emma's parents any further today?"

"I made a couple of calls and found that her mother used to be stationed in Massachusetts before deploying to Iraq, but I wasn't able to reach anyone at the base who would tell me anything yet." Josh took a bite and chewed thoughtfully, "I think I'm going to give another old buddy of mine a call. He's been moving up the ranks pretty steadily since he enlisted, so he may be able to get me in touch with someone who will actually tell me something of value."

They finished their lunch and gave the girls their treats, then Olivia stood up.

"I'm thinking of going by the thrift stores to see what goodies I can find from my clients' lists. I've been really bad about looking for their items that I'm going to lose all my clientele if I don't get it together," Olivia smiled ruefully, referring to the clients who paid her to find specific antiques and vintage items for them.

"Why don't you leave the girls here with me then," Josh volunteered. "It'll make your life easier and they'll enjoy hanging out here more than sitting in the car."

"Okay, thank," she stretched her back and gathered up her purse. "Have fun girls."

Josh kissed her goodbye and she locked the door behind her.

I should ask around about that con man while I'm out too, she thought, as she started the car. *It wouldn't surprise me if he was trying to hit up other women for money too.*

There was only one other car in the lot by the tiny thrift store at the end of town when Olivia parked. She knew that would be her friend Diane's, who managed the shop.

"Hi Twiggy," Olivia bent to scoop up the barking Chihuahua as she entered the shop. "Hey, Diane, How's it going?"

"Liv, long time, no see," Diane smiled as she walked from the other room. "How are the wedding preparations going?"

"They're going," Olivia laughed. "It's amazing how hectic it is getting married."

"Well, I for one, can't wait to see what you've done with that old mansion in Birchwood. Aren't you even a little worried that it might be haunted?"

Olivia smiled, wondering what Diane would think if she knew they'd also purchased the purportedly haunted house, in which Thomas Jacobson had been killed, for their new office. "No, I'm sure Edna Hill is resting in peace now, since her murder was solved. The house feels at peace too, if you know what I mean. It turned out to be really beautiful."

"Yes, I guess that would have put her spirit to rest. Oh, I have a really nice set of copper bottom pots and pans I think you'd like. I don't know if they're on your list, but I'll bet you won't turn them down, either way," the large woman chortled, heading to the small kitchen area of the shop to retrieve them.

"Oh my stars, they're stunning," Olivia breathed. "You can be sure I won't be turning them down." She took a large skillet in her hands, turning it over to see if there

118

were dents or deep scratches. "They are in beautiful shape. Thanks so much for holding them for me."

"I knew you'd appreciate them more than anyone I could think of," she smiled, wrapping each of them up carefully in paper and placing them all in a bag. "That'll be twenty dollars."

"Perfect" Olivia smiled happily, forking over the money and heading over to the walls to look at the other items displayed around the shop. "If I can leave them here, I want to see what other cool things you've gotten since I was here last."

"No worries, Liv, you can leave it as long as you want," Diane ran her hand though her short brown hair and fanned herself with some paper, "Is it too warm in here? I've been having hot flashes lately, so I'm never sure if it's the temperature or just me."

"Oh, that's something I am not looking forward to," Olivia grimaced. "It feels fine in here to me, so that may be a flash."

"Ugh," the older woman laughed, "I had a feeling. Well, at least I know, so I won't be freezing poor Twiggy out by turning off the heat. I'll just step outside now and then to cool off."

Olivia grinned, then gasped as she saw a gorgeous little taupe colored Wedgwood Jasperware bowl. She looked it over quickly, hearing the outer door open. No chips, scratches or anything that she could see. One of her clients was going to be really happy.

As she scanned the other room, looking for hidden treasures, she could hear Diane talking with another woman who'd obviously just entered the shop. The other voice sounded agitated.

Grabbing a sweet old porcelain doll for Emma, to add to her purchases, Olivia walked back into the main room.

The woman looked up and Olivia could see that her eyes were red, as though she'd been crying recently.

"Hi Gladys, are you okay?" Olivia asked solicitously.

"I'm okay Olivia, but my mom, she did something really crazy and I don't know how to help her." The young woman's blue eyes filled with tears. "I had to tell Aunt Diane, to see if she had any ideas."

Diane had sat down and was shaking her head, looking almost ill.

"What happened, Gladys? What did she do?" Olivia had a feeling she already knew.

"She gave away most of her money to some man who promised her a pretty cottage on the lake." Gladys sniffled, "She said she was going to give it to me for a wedding present when Gary and I get married in June. The cottage didn't even belong to that man. It was all a trick, and now she barely has any money left for herself."

Diane got up and took her niece in her arms, as she broke down in sobs.

"What can I do to help my mom?" Gladys wailed. "She did it for me, and he robbed her."

Olivia sighed heavily, "Josh and I will do our best to find him, Gladys. We're already looking for him, since he's done the same thing to someone else. Right now, if you can bring your mom to our office and have her bring any papers he gave her so we can find out everything she knows about him, that's the best place to start. Don't worry; there won't be any fee for this. Josh is there now, and I'm on my way as soon as I pay for these."

"I'll go get her now," Gladys promised, sniffling and then blowing her nose. "Thank you so much, Olivia." she sniffed one last time and hurried out the door.

"Thanks Olivia, my sister is a sweet lady, but she can be way too trusting and foolish with her money sometimes," Diane sat back down.

"No, don't blame your sister this time. This man is very good at conning people, I'm afraid." She handed the Wedgwood piece and the doll to Diane and took out her wallet again.

"Not a chance, Liv," Diane waved her money away. "You're helping my family, and your money is no good here." She quickly wrapped the two items and put them in a separate bag from the pots and pans.

Olivia thanked her, said goodbye to her and Twiggy, and hurried out with her bags, to make sure she reached the office before Gladys and her mom, so she'd have a chance to explain it all to Josh first.

Josh was both elated at the new information, and discouraged that yet another person had been victimized by the con artist.

"I hope she has something we can use to help us find this creep, Roger Manning, or whatever his name is. We need to get her to report this to the Birchwood PD too, Josh fumed. "I want this guy off the streets."

"Right there with you, Josh," Olivia said sadly. "It's hard seeing people get ripped off like this. I feel so badly for Elaine and Gladys' mom, Donna, too. Being conned makes people feel stupid and hopeless, and that makes me furious at that guy."

Gladys and her mother arrived soon after Olivia had finished talking to Josh about the case. Olivia let them in and introduced them to Josh, who they had never met before. Donna's eyes were even more red-rimmed than her daughter's, so it was easy to see how upset she was by the whole thing.

Molly and Sheyna seemed to sense that the women needed comforting and made themselves available for pets and snuggles.

Donna, especially seemed to appreciate Molly's attention, rubbing her fur and seeming to draw strength from it as she recounted her tale.

It turned out that the man, who'd again given his name as Roger Manning, had pulled an almost identical scam on Donna as he had on Elaine. She'd met the man in the post office queue, waiting to mail a parcel, and he'd struck up a conversation, telling her he was sending a package to his daughter for her birthday.

After they had both finished mailing their packages, he escorted her out to her car, and they continued talking. He asked her what she did for a living, and volunteered that he was a realtor, and was really excited over a little lakeside cottage he'd just been given to list, that was priced really low, since the sellers were desperate for the money.

She'd fallen for it, hook, line and sinker, much to her chagrin. She begged Josh and Olivia to find him and get the money back, or at least keep him from swindling anyone else.

Josh and Olivia promised to do their best, and were able to persuade her and Gladys to go to the police department right away and report the incident. Donna was embarrassed, but after a little encouragement, agreed to go straight there.

"Well, that wasn't much help, unfortunately," Josh remarked glumly. "I'd really hoped for at least one new lead, but it was almost the same story verbatim."

Olivia raised her head suddenly from petting Sheyna, "Except where they met . . . she met him at the post office . . . standing in line." Her eyes took on a look of hope, "Josh, the post office has cameras that record everything going on in the room. Maybe we can get them to let us look at the videos, or if not us, then the police department."

"Liv, you're a genius," Josh grabbed her and twirled her around. "Maybe we can finally get a picture out to all the cops and nail this guy."

Olivia laughed and hugged Josh as he set her down, "I'm definitely not a genius, but I do have a fairly good memory, and I noticed the cameras a while back when I was bored waiting for service."

"I'll call the post office first and see if they'll allow us to see the tape, if they refuse, maybe you should call Julie and let her get her Chief to call. I have a feeling they'll cooperate with him." Josh looked happier than he had all day, dialing the number.

"Well, I guess you need to call Julie, because he said it isn't legal for him to let us look at it, but agreed that the cops could take the tape if they asked for it." He scoffed as he ended the call.

"I figured as much," Olivia said, reaching for her phone. "The post office is definitely a stickler for the rules."

A couple of minutes later, Olivia ended the call with a faint smirk on her face.

"Yay, Julie! Her boss said we can watch the tape too, since we've been so good about sharing with them and got Donna to report the scam to them, when she wouldn't have otherwise."

"Yes!" Josh pumped a fist in the air laughing. "Birchwood PD is awesome! I don't care what kind of silly rivalry we may have had when I was a state trooper."

Olivia laughed with him, "Okay Mr. Alpha Cop, let's go to the police station and see this tape already. The girls can stay here while we're gone."

The Chief of Police was there, and shook their hands, as he led them into the room where they could all sit and watch the tape.

At first it looked like the man might have been aware of the cameras and kept his head turned on purpose, but finally, as the line moved up, he and Donna both turned for a moment, as a lady in front of them dropped a package. His overtly gallant gesture of quickly picking it up and making sure she had hold of it, might prove to be his undoing, as his face was shown quite clearly.

Everyone in the room cheered, as Julie froze the tape. The Chief ordered that frame to be printed and distributed to all the officers, and copies emailed to the other PDs in the area, including the state police. Josh and Olivia were given copies as well.

"Well, that will be a big help," Josh smiled broadly. "We need to keep our eyes peeled for this guy and hope we see him before he swindles anyone else, or decides to move on from the area."

"Yeah, that's what worries me," Olivia frowned. "I don't really know much about how con artists operate, but I'd imagine they wouldn't stay in one area for very long, as it would get awfully hot for them, wouldn't it?"

"Yes, especially in small towns like these," Josh agreed. "I doubt he'll stay around much longer, so we need to find him fast."

"I've got to stop by the grocery store in town before I go home, so I'll be watching as I drive and, of course, while I'm there," Olivia smiled. "Is there anything special you'd like for dinner the next couple of days?"

"Ooh, now that you mention it, I'd love some of that awesome eggplant no parm that you make," Josh wagged his eyebrows and smiled broadly. "That is one of my all-time favorites of your recipes."

Olivia grinned, "Vicki's grandmother, Maria, gave me that recipe. I love it too, and it's about time Emma and Sophia tried eggplant. I'll bet they've never had it."

"I'll bet you're right, especially Sophia," Josh chuckled. "I've never seen eggplant flavored baby food, and she wasn't even eating any other solid food when we got her . . . except maybe mushed bananas."

"I hope they like it. Eggplant can be an acquired taste for some people, but if they start eating it now, they should get used to it quickly."

"If they're ever going to like eggplant, it will be in that recipe," Josh praised her. "My mouth is watering, just thinking about it."

"Well, that will definitely be tonight's dinner, then." Olivia blushed at the praise. "I need to order more Vegeta soon; I think I'm getting low, but I certainly have enough for tonight," she added hastily, laughing, as she saw Josh's face fall. "Mam always said men were ruled by their stomachs."

"Among other things," Josh chuckled, tongue in cheek. "But I *am* relieved that you aren't out of the Ve-whatever-it's-called."

Olivia swatted at him playfully with the papers in her hand. "Well, at least your stomach will be taken care of tonight."

They were both grinning as they got into Josh's SUV and headed back to the office.

"I'll bring Molly and Sheyna home with me, when I come for dinner," Josh offered, "That way they don't have to wait in the car at the grocery store. I'll even take them for a nice walk here in town so you don't have to worry about a big walk later."

"Oh my, you really are looking forward to the eggplant, aren't you?" Olivia teased. "Thanks, Josh. That will be a big help."

Josh parked in the tiny lot by their office and Olivia kissed him quickly before hopping out and climbing into her own SUV, as he walked up the steps into the office.

The grocery store wasn't very crowded, so Olivia grabbed the ingredients needed for the evening meal, as well as the few other things from her list and quickly went through the checkout.

As she left the store, she heard a crashing sound from around the corner toward the parking lot. She and a woman who'd been behind her, coming out the door, hurried to see what had happened.

Olivia gasped and swayed, almost dropping the groceries, as she saw that her windshield had been shattered. She forgot for a second that Molly and Sheyna were safely at the office with Josh. She heard the sound of screeching tires, as someone sped away down the road from behind the store.

She rushed to her car, the woman following her, along with a few more people who had run from the store to see what the noise was all about.

Setting the bags of food down on the pavement, Olivia carefully peeked inside her car to see a baseball bat with a paper wrapped around the center of it lying on the front seat.

She quickly dialed 911 and after telling the dispatcher what had happened, she called Josh.

The people gathered around, began to offer assistance when she hung up, and she had to stop a couple of them from reaching inside to retrieve the bat, as she knew there was a slight possibility that there were fingerprints on it.

The store workers soon reluctantly went back inside, leaving only three or four people who seemed intent upon staying to watch whatever further excitement may occur until the police arrived.

The police were there very quickly, with Josh only five minutes behind them, the latter clearly having done a fair bit of speeding to get there so fast.

Josh parked right next to Olivia's car, Molly and Sheyna sitting in their crates in the back of his SUV. He gathered the abandoned grocery bags, and put them in the backseat of his car, then stood with an arm around Olivia while they watched the police officers examining the mess of glass and the baseball bat.

Luckily for them, Julie was one of the cops at the scene, and she quickly motioned for them to come over, as she carefully spread the paper out with gloved hands to see what it said.

"*'You'd best let sleeping murders lie, or you may be the next to die,'*" Josh read over her shoulder.

"Wow," Julie chuckled dryly, "You really do have a stalker who fancies himself a poet."

"A stalker or a murderer," Olivia murmured. "I'm pretty sure this isn't just ordinary stalking, Jules. You know, I've been looking into the murder of that lawyer, Jacobson, from fifty years ago, besides the con artist."

"I might have believed in one coincidence, but not two," Josh added. "Julie, this is definitely aimed at Olivia because of that old murder, not the swindling case, and not just a stalker. I mean, read what this note says, poetry aside."

"I think you're right, guys," Julie agreed. "It does mention murder, so you must be getting onto something, Liv. You should start being more careful from this point on."

"I'm still shaking at the thought that I almost had Molly and Sheyna with me. Josh, if you hadn't offered to bring them home later, they could have been injured." Olivia hugged him again, then went to see the girls in their crates, as if reassuring herself that they were all right.

"She's right, you know," Josh said to Julie. "This is getting dangerous. Anything you can do to help keep her safe, will be appreciated."

"Josh, you know I'll do whatever I can. I'm on the night shift right now, so I won't be home with her at night, but I can manage to drive by the house now and then and maybe get one of the others to do the same."

"Thanks, Julie," Josh scratched his head thoughtfully. "I think I'm going to hire an off duty officer to watch over the house in the day time for a while, and another one to patrol the outside of the house at night, so you don't have to worry about doing that. I appreciate it, but I wasn't thinking about the fact that it could get you in trouble with your Chief."

"Thanks, Josh. I'll still poke my nose by whenever I am in the area just to make sure your hired guy is there and all looks well." Julie offered with a grin. "I love Livvie and the girls too. Liv is the sister I never had."

Olivia came back in time to hear the last sentence. "Aww, Julie, I feel the same about you. It's going to be strange not having you in the same house once we move."

"At least we'll only be a few miles apart. I promise to visit often enough that you'll wish I lived further away," Julie laughed. "Not until you newlyweds have had some time to yourselves though.

"Okay, let me get this back to the station, and I'll let you know if there are any prints on it." Julie bagged the paper with the threatening message on it and walked over to another officer, motioning to him to collect the bat carefully.

"I'll call a wrecker to take your car to the glass place so they can replace the windshield," Josh took his cell phone and dialed, as they walked back to his car. "We can go straight home from here, since I locked up the office already. I'll go home after dinner, then come back in the morning to give you a ride to pick up your car."

"Thanks, Josh; that sounds like a great plan." Olivia smiled gratefully, as she climbed into the SUV. "You have no idea how thankful I am that the girls were with you. That glass flew all the way back into their crates."

"I'll call and get someone to clean the SUV and crates out thoroughly too after the glass is replaced, so it will be ready to drive when we pick it up." Josh noted. "You certainly can't use it with glass all over it like that."

Olivia grinned as she sat back for the ride home, "You've definitely earned that dinner, Josh. You really didn't need to work so hard for it."

Josh's shoulders shook, and he snorted with laughter, "Babe, you scare the skin off me sometimes. Who else could possibly generate so much excitement going to the grocery store?"

"Yep, I can never resist putting on a show," Olivia joked, letting go of the tension in laughter.

"I'm so glad you were inside and the girls were with me when it happened," Josh said sobering. "I'm scared half to death sometimes thinking of the crazy things that happen to you in these investigations. It's like you have a scary nutcase magnet hidden on you somewhere."

"It scares me silly sometimes too, Josh. It isn't like I go looking for these things to happen, you know."

"That's the part that's the scariest, Liv. You don't even have to look for it–it looks for you." Josh shook his head ruefully. "You seem to get into more danger than I *ever* did when I was a cop."

"Well, hopefully we can solve this murder case quickly and get life back to normal," Olivia said seriously. "I'm not fond of having to look over my shoulder or worrying about my loved ones either."

"Should we stop and pick up something for dinner, so you don't have to cook?" Josh asked solicitously. "That had to have been pretty unnerving."

Olivia laughed, "No, Josh. You're definitely getting your eggplant no parm. It would take more than that to keep me from making your favorite food after you saved my girls."

"That wasn't a hint, Livvie," Josh laughed. "I just didn't want you to feel obligated to cook, after having such a lousy experience. I'd truly be fine with picking up something to go."

"No way, I'm fine with cooking tonight. Now, if you asked me to run a relay race, that might be problematic, but cooking, that's relaxing."

Josh carried the groceries into the house when they arrived and Molly and Sheyna raced into the house, almost tripping Emma, as she and Sophia ran to greet them and Olivia and Josh.

They soon had the groceries sorted out, and Olivia tried to talk Annie into staying for dinner, but she had already told Abby that she was going to watch a movie with her, so she declined, hurrying home to change before Abby arrived.

Emma helped Josh set the table and Sophia carried the spoons and set them on the edge of the table. While Olivia prepared the eggplant for the oven, Molly carried her bowl to Josh, who then mixed hers and Sheyna's food and handed the bowls to Emma and Sophia, who carefully set them in their designated places. Sheyna supervised purrfectly, as only a cat could.

Olivia smiled warmly, as she watched her little family, all working together to make dinner go smoothly.

"Such teamwork," she praised them. "Work is so much more fun when it's shared. Emma, you and Sophia are getting very good at helping."

"I like helping you Aunt Livvie," Emma smiled widely, her brown eyes shining. "And I'm getting so big, I can set the table almost all by myself."

"I heppin too," Sophia said proudly.

"Yes you were, Sophia," Olivia smiled at the little girl, "You did the spoons all by yourself. You and Emma are awesome helpers and I am really proud of you both."

"Speaking of helpers," Josh chuckled ruefully, ruffling both little girls' hair as he passed by, "I'm going to call Dave Johnson, to see if he's available to watch the house for a while, so please excuse me while I take Molly out back to do her business, so I can call in private."

Olivia sighed, remembering when Dave, the security guard friend of Josh, had been hired to watch her house several months ago, when she had another murderer who was threatening hers and Molly's and Sheyna's safety.

Josh's old friend was a good guy and Olivia decided to add another eggplant to the meal, just in case he said yes. Dave loved home cooking. She could always take him a plate later if he came to watch the place once Josh left for the night. She was sure he wouldn't mind a late night snack.

The dinner turned out perfectly. Emma and Sophia, after looking puzzled at the taste and texture of the eggplant, decided it was good after all, and ate a pretty large piece of it between them. Josh was so busy eating that he was much quieter than usual.

After dinner, the whole family went for a short walk, with Josh carrying Sophia and Sheyna both after the first few minutes, while Olivia and Emma chatted away, with Molly in the lead.

Olivia was grateful that her daughters didn't notice her missing SUV, as she really didn't want to have to explain what had happened.

Once the little girls were in bed and Molly was snoozing by the fire, Josh and Olivia sat back and talked about the cases for a little while, trying to fit some of the pieces together.

"The brick and bat throwing poet has to be related to the old murder." Olivia scoffed, "How does he even know I'm investigating it?"

"It *is* a small town, Livvie," Josh chuckled. "You know exactly how that goes."

"Yeah, I guess I do," she grinned, "I've been using it to my advantage since the beginning of this investigation, asking questions at all the most likely gossip points. I guess it works both ways."

"Yep, all the old men at Spots, the ladies at the beauty shop . . . not to mention the librarian and anyone who might have heard you asking about the old murder there . . . you can bet they spread that around like wildfire." Josh shook his head with a grin. "Nothing like a small town for lightning fast news relay."

"Even some of the folks at the retirement center may have been talking to their visitors about all my questions," Olivia made a face. "I'm not sure why I don't expect the whole county to know when I'm looking into something as exciting as a murder, even a very old one."

"Well, Dave will be here soon, and I'll be able to sleep better tonight knowing he's watching over you guys." Josh hugged her, and she snuggled into him for a kiss. They laughed when Sheyna flicked her tail in annoyance, as Olivia crowded her space on Josh's lap.

"Okay, Sheyna girl, I have to get up now anyway," Josh rubbed the cat's head as he lifted her to the back on the couch and stood, stretching, with a yawn. "It's been a busy day."

"That's for sure," Olivia seconded, rising to accompany him to the door. "Oh, wait, Josh. I have a piece of the eggplant for Dave, if you don't mind taking it out to him," she smiled, spotting the guard's inconspicuous sedan parked by the road.

"He'll be even happier about accepting my offer on such short notice," Josh laughed. "There's nothing like getting wonderful free home cooked meals on top of good pay."

Olivia watched as Josh handed Dave the plate through the car window. Dave waved an enthusiastic 'thank you' and the two men talked for a moment, then she waved to them, and closed the door as Josh drove away.

She took Molly out for a quick trip in the back yard, then checked on the sleeping children, kissing them both again, as she headed to her own bedroom.

Molly and Sheyna followed her to her bed and all three were sound asleep within minutes.

CHAPTER ELEVEN

The next week flew by so fast Olivia felt like she'd never have everything ready in time for the wedding. She had only two weeks left now and her parents and her mother's parents were coming in a week. She knew that no matter how much help they may be in getting things done, that invariably, things would feel more hectic with them there, simply because there would be so many people living in a small space, and they would be trying to get to know Josh and the children too.

There hadn't been any new breaks or developments in either of the cases, and she and Josh were both feeling a little frustrated over that, as well as being worried that the poetic pitcher, as Julie had started calling the brick and bat thrower, might strike again.

Olivia waved goodbye to the little girls and Annie as Annie backed out of the driveway with the kids in the backseat in their car seats. Annie was meeting Abby, and they were taking the children to an alpaca farm for the day where they could pet and play with the animals. Both little girls were very excited.

Olivia put Molly's and Sheyna's harnesses on and loaded them into their crates in the SUV, which was all cleaned out, with a sparkling new windshield. Molly pranced excitedly in her crate, knowing they were going to do their retirement center visit.

Pam greeted Olivia with a happy smile, letting her know that Julie and the two cats, the soon-to-be-resident needed a home for, had fallen in love with each other, and Julie and their current person had gotten along really well too, so there was going to be a happy ending to that story.

"I am so glad you came up with the idea of the foster/adoption with visitation rights for these people and their pets," Pam beamed at her. "The new people will be so much happier, knowing they can still see their pets frequently."

"What happens if they become too frail to visit?" Olivia asked hesitantly. "Could I volunteer to bring the pets to them, if I make sure they are well behaved enough? I know it's technically against the rules, if they aren't certified therapy animals, but . . . ."

"Yes, it is against the rules, but I trust your judgment, so if you guarantee their behavior, I'll make sure I don't see you bring them in," Pam chortled, "I am all for making the people's lives better whenever possible."

"Thanks, Pam. You're a peach," Olivia hugged her friend. "So, I'm going to start with Mrs. Martin, and end with Mr. Turner, catching Mr. Adams, Mrs. Barnes and a couple of others in between."

"Sounds like a plan," Pam agreed. "Mr. Turner is wonderful, and though he is a really kind man, I think he is quite lonely. He hasn't had a single visitor since he arrived."

"Have he and Mrs. Martin gotten to talk to each other much?" Olivia wrinkled her brow. "I have a feeling they'd get on great."

"I haven't noticed them together at all, so I doubt they've really talked beyond possibly a casual meeting."

"Would it be possible for me to introduce them? I'm not trying to play matchmaker, but I think they'd be a very likely pair to be friends."

"Great idea," Pam's face lit up. "I think both of them could use a good friend in here. Why don't you invite them to come to the crafts room, since it is unoccupied at this hour? You and the girls can visit with them both at the same time and they'll get to meet, if they haven't yet. Knowing you, you will all discuss the murder too." Pam laughed, as Olivia grinned guiltily.

"You got me," she laughed. "Mrs. Martin said she was Miss Jane Marple, from Agatha Christy's books and I was Zoe Donovan, from Kathi Daley's books, so I guess Mr. Turner can be Hercule Poirot, unless he has a favorite detective he'd rather be."

Pam laughed, "You guys are a riot. I can see you and your merry little band of sleuths solving it too. I'll make sure the room is unlocked for you. Have fun." She petted Molly and Sheyna before heading down the hallway.

Olivia decided to visit the other people on her list first, saving Mrs. Martin and Mr. Turner for last.

Mrs. Barnes, who'd had to leave her cat behind when she moved in several months ago, was as delighted as always to see Sheyna. She called her Mona a few times, which had been her cat's name, but Sheyna didn't mind a bit, and happily purred against her rubbing hand.

Once they'd finished with all the other visits, Olivia stopped by Mrs. Martin's room and asked if she felt up to meeting Mr. Turner, and if she minded including him in their little sleuthing band, telling her that Pam had thought he was lonely.

Mrs. Martin was happy with the idea of meeting him and said she'd already noticed him and found him interesting.

"He seems like a nice, intelligent man, and we all need friends in here," she said, as she slipped her sweater on over the light dress she was wearing. "It's always cooler in the crafts room than in the bedrooms, you know."

She, Olivia and the girls walked together to the crafts room. Mrs. Martin waited there, so Olivia could ask Mr. Turner if he was amenable to the meeting in private, rather than causing embarrassment for anyone if he wasn't.

Fortunately, Mr. Turner thought it was a wonderful idea. He seemed quite excited about properly meeting Mrs. Martin, since he had noticed her and thought she seemed interesting as well as attractive, and also rather excited about discussing an old murder case.

Olivia introduced the two elderly people, and as everyone sat and made themselves comfortable, with Molly's head in Mrs. Martin's lap and Sheyna purring happily in Mr. Turner's lap, Olivia ran through the basics of what she knew about the fifty-year-old murder.

"Wow, you've had someone throwing bricks and baseball bats wrapped in bad poetry at you?" Mr. Turner looked taken aback. "That's a bit beyond the pale, isn't it?"

Olivia laughed, "Just a bit. I'm seriously hoping we can catch him before he throws any more of them. This case is getting to be a lot less fun, now that I have to keep looking over my shoulder all the time."

"You solved another old murder, a few months ago, didn't you?" he asked. "I think it was you that I read about in the paper."

"Yes, with the help of my fiancé, Josh, and Molly and Sheyna, as well as other people," Olivia blushed, slightly. "Josh used to be a Lieutenant Detective with the State Police, so he was a huge help."

"She and Josh have started their own detective agency now, Mountain Valley Investigations, right, Livvie?" Mrs. Martin offered proudly. "They have already solved their first official murder case, as well as a couple of others before they even had the agency."

"I'm honored to be allowed to help in any way I can," Mr. Turner said gallantly, looking delighted. "I've always been a mystery buff."

"Well then, you are welcome to assume the persona of your favorite detective, if you like," Mrs. Martin chuckled softly, "I've decided to be Miss Jane Marple, and I assigned the role of Zoe Donovan, from another of our favorite series to Olivia."

"Then I suppose I shall be Tommy Beresford, though I must say, I think you're a lot more like Tuppence than Miss Marple. Perhaps you could be persuaded to change your mind at some point?" Mr. Turner suggested, with a twinkle in his eye, obviously quite taken with Mrs. Martin, who blushed slightly, as she smiled at him.

"Perhaps . . . I was always fond of Tommy and Tuppence as well," she answered, clearing her throat. "So, Olivia, what other news do you have for us?"

Olivia grinned slightly, noting the subtle undercurrents flowing between her two fellow sleuths. "Well, there haven't really been any new developments on the murder case since I spoke with you last, Mrs. Martin, aside from the poetry laden baseball bat. I *did* want to alert you both to the fact that there is a con man operating in the area, so please be extra careful if anyone is trying to sell you anything."

They both assured her they would be vigilant, and Olivia was pretty sure that both were astute enough to not fall for a con man's tricks easily.

"My family is coming in from Ireland next week for the wedding, and I am so excited to see them," Olivia smiled. "I know Mam and Da will want to come and visit with you Mrs. Martin. Mr. Turner, did you know my parents, Patrick and Brigid McKenna? They used to live here before moving back to Ireland to stay with my Mam's parents."

"I knew Paddy McKenna, who used to live in Birchwood, is that your father?" he answered thoughtfully.

"Yes, that's my Da," Olivia grinned. "Did you get on with him well?"

"Oh yes, I liked him a lot. He was great friends with my son until he and your mother moved away. I'd forgotten where they went, but it makes sense they went to Ireland. You mother was born there, right?"

"Born and raised," Olivia agreed. "My grandparents still live there. Mam and Da moved there a few years ago, since Nana and Pop needed a little help in their old age."

"I'll be looking forward to seeing them again," Mr. Turner exclaimed. "It's been quite a while."

"I will too," Mrs. Martin chimed in. "I've missed chatting with your Mam over the years, Livvie. She was always one to brighten my day. Will Mona be coming by too?"

"I'm sure she will, and maybe Pop too. I'd forgotten you'd met Nana and Pop. You all went to dinner several times when they last visited, if I'm remembering right."

"Yes, we had a wonderful time, and Mona and Críostóir made Ireland sound so beautiful, Don and I had planned to visit them the next year," her eyes took on a hint of sadness. "Unfortunately, he became ill a few months later, so we never got to do that."

Mr. Turner gave her a look of sympathy and petted her hand, "I'm so sorry for your loss."

"Thank you. It's been over fourteen years, but I still miss him." She straightened her shoulders, "So Olivia, I'm sure you must be needing to get back to your wedding preparations, rather than hanging around a couple of old people."

"There are few people I'd rather hang around with, Mrs. Martin, whatever your ages," Olivia hugged her, causing Molly to cock her head inquiringly. "You've always been one of my favorite people, and I have a feeling Mr. Turner, is about to join that club as well as joining our sleuthing club." She smiled at them. "Speaking of that, Mr. Turner, I'd be honored if you would attend my wedding. Mrs. Martin is hopefully already planning to come, and I think Pam can fit you into her car as well, if you'd like to come."

"I'm the one who'd be honored, and delighted." He shook Olivia's hand. "Please accept my congratulations and my acceptance of your kind invitation."

"I'm so happy you're both coming. Yes, I suppose I had better get back to work on the preparations, now that you mention it, but I will be back next week, and hopefully with Mam, Da, Nana and Pop in tow."

"I'll try to discretely question some of the other residents to see if anyone has further information about the murder in the meantime," Mr. Turner volunteered.

"If you do, please be very careful," Olivia cautioned. "It is a murderer we're dealing with, and I don't want either of you to put yourselves in harm's way."

"I'll be careful, and I'll watch over Miss Jane slash Tuppence as well. I can't allow my lovely new friend to fall afoul of the murderer either," he stated gallantly, with a warm smile at Mrs. Martin.

Olivia hugged them both and gathered Molly and Sheyna's leashes in hand to go and find Pam. She watched with a smile as Mr. Turner escorted Mrs. Martin to her room.

After making sure that Pam was amenable to bringing Mr. Turner to the wedding as well as Mrs. Martin, Olivia promised to come back the following week, bringing her Ireland relatives along to visit their old friends.

I think I'll take the girls home and give them a nice walk in the park on the way, then maybe I'll try the courthouse to see if there are any records of old cases in which Jacobson was the attorney, Olivia thought to herself. *It looks like it may snow later, so Sheyna will be much happier if she gets her walk before that.*

The park was fairly deserted, with just a few people walking around the sparsely snow covered ground, so it was quite peaceful. Olivia felt her spirit calming and her tension ebbing away as the snow crunched under their feet. The girls enjoyed their walk as well, Molly trotting briskly ahead, to dash back playfully, while Sheyna eyed a couple of winter birds who watched her warily from the leaf bare trees.

All too soon, the chill began to permeate her thin jacket, since she hadn't dressed for being outside, so sighing, Olivia led the girls back to the SUV and loaded them into their crates.

"Sorry, girls, I wish I'd thought to wear a heavier coat, we could have had a longer walk, but I'm freezing in this thing."

Sheyna nuzzled her hand for another pet, before Olivia closed her crate door, and Olivia obliged her, giving Molly a few extra pets too.

Driving through town, Olivia's eyes popped open wide as she spotted a familiar face. *Could it be . . .?* She double checked to make sure her eyes weren't playing tricks on her, before calling Josh to report the immediate whereabouts of the con man they'd been searching for.

She stealthily followed him with her car, keeping on the side of the road, well behind him so he wouldn't notice her until Josh arrived.

Josh immediately jumped out of his car and accosted the man, holding him until Julie drove up in her police car.

Josh informed the man that one of the people he'd swindled was the mother of a police officer, so if he wanted things to go better for him, he'd be best off returning all the money he'd gotten from the people in this town.

The man agreed to do so, if Josh would put in a good word with the cops and the prosecutor, so it seemed that both Elaine and Donna would get their money back, as well as possibly other victims they didn't yet know of.

Josh congratulated Olivia on spotting the man and keeping him in sight until he could be caught.

She informed him of her plan to go to the courthouse, so he agreed to head to the police station and make a statement, so she could continue on her way.

The temperatures were dropping and Olivia could almost smell the snow in the air by the time they arrived home, so she hurriedly got the girls settled in the house, promising to be back soon, and left for the courthouse. She wanted to be back before the dark and the impending snow made her return trip more dangerous. She knew there might be quite a few tourists and out of state skiers on the road later who might not know how to drive in snowy conditions, especially in the dark, so it was better not to give them a target.

Olivia took the back roads out of town and down to the courthouse as much as possible, but on the other side of North Conway, there was still a little more traffic than she'd have liked, so it took her close to an hour to get there.

Once she was in the building, it took her a while to figure out where to go to research old court cases. She finally discovered that she needed to go to the building next door which housed the records.

Before leaving the courthouse, she peeked into a few rooms, where hearings and trials seemed to be occurring, but stopped, self consciously after noting that everyone in the rooms turned to look at her when she opened the doors.

Yikes, you'd think they could spare a little oil for those squeaky hinges, she thought wryly.

As she left the building, she passed a heavy set elderly man, wearing a heavy parka with a hood over a suit. His face was partially covered by a wool scarf, but she noticed his pale blue eyes go wide under bushy white eyebrows, as he looked up at her. He startled and quickly turned his head away from her.

She nodded and said hello, but the man hurried past her, glancing over his shoulder furtively before entering the building.

Olivia almost tripped over the final step, as she watched the man's odd behavior.

What on earth . . .? She shook her head in perplexity as she continued toward the smaller building that housed the court records. *Could that have been the murderer? Maybe I should go back and try to get a better look at him.*

She stopped and stood indecisively for a few moments, before finally heading toward the records building after all. *If it was the murderer, I will have definitely lost the advantage of surprise. If I go looking for him, he'll be on the lookout as well, and since I only saw his eyes, I'd never recognize him unless he did something to call attention to himself. I can't just go staring at every older man in the building. I should have followed him right away,"* she berated herself.

Feeling disgusted with herself, Olivia entered the small building, and asked where she could research old court records. She sat for the next hour, blurring her eyes with microfilm.

There were a lot of cases in which Jacobson had been the attorney of record, and Olivia didn't have time to go through all of them carefully, so she skimmed them as best she could, looking for something to jump out at her.

She saw the case involving the drunk driver who'd killed Matty Phillips and it confirmed that he'd been fined and sentenced to only six months in the county jail, as Mrs. Martin had told her. The presiding judge was the Honorable George Pane.

Olivia shook her head at the ruling, wondering how he could have given out such a light sentence for not only killing someone while driving drunk, but then driving away without even calling for help.

If he hadn't gone off the road a few miles past Matty's almost crushed car with the tree embedded in the windshield, and gotten stuck in the ditch, they might never have known who had hit her, but fortunately for her family, he had. That tiny speck of good fortune for the family in the whole tragic affair hadn't gone as far as getting a just sentence for their daughter's killer. He'd apparently paid his fine, served his six months and gone his merry way back out of state, leaving Matty's parents to grieve for the rest of their lives.

I could sympathize with Charles Phillips, if he'd killed the man who'd run Matty off the road into a tree, or even the judge who'd passed the unfair sentence, but why would he kill the lawyer? Olivia still couldn't make sense of that scenario, try as she might.

Back to perusing the microfilm, she searched until her eyes rebelled, not finding anything else of note. *I'll have to come back again soon; I didn't get halfway through the cases.* She sighed and put it away, cleaning up the area she'd used and putting away her all too brief notes.

CHAPTER TWELVE

The sun was moving close to the horizon in the west as she drove home, and she had to turn on her wipers halfway home, as the snow started and very quickly became a heavy swirling chaos against her windshield.

It started as a wet snow, plastering itself to the road and soon creating hazardous driving conditions, but luckily, as she drove higher toward home, the air was a little colder and the snow, drier, so she made it safely.

Annie's car was parked in the driveway, along with Josh's SUV. Olivia's face lit up, at the knowledge that her loved ones were home safe.

Josh opened the door, just before she could touch the knob, and took her in his arms.

"I was just about to call you," he said in a relieved sounding voice. "I got here a couple of minutes ago, and when you weren't here I started to get worried. You didn't have any more trouble, did you?"

"No, I'm fine," she murmured against his coat. "I went to both the courthouse and the records department of the county building to do some research, and the driving was slow and tricky on the way back."

Emma and Sophia were in the kitchen, helping Annie cook dinner when Olivia and Josh walked in.

"Mama wook, I hep," Sophia said proudly, carrying a handful of spoons toward the table. She put one spoon beside each plate carefully, then turned and ran to hug Olivia's legs.

Olivia grinned broadly, and picked her up, smothering her face in kisses. The little girl laughed as Olivia made her kisses loud and smoochy.

Emma finished setting the knives and forks on the table where they belonged before she joined her sister in hugging Olivia and Josh.

"We had so much fun!" she announced happily. Aunt Annie and Aunt Abby took us to see Alpacas and we got to pet them and we got to ride a pony and everything."

"I pet pacas," Sophia beamed, flinging herself into Josh's arms from Olivia's and startling both adults in the process.

"Yikes, Sophia, you could have fallen on your head," Olivia scolded mildly. "It's okay to reach for Daddy or to ask him to take you, but you mustn't lunge like that. It's dangerous."

Sophia pouted for a second, then forgot to be upset, and bounced up and down in Josh's arms. "I wide pony too," she yelled in renewed excitement.

Everyone laughed as the little girl bounced in Josh's arms like he was the pony.

"Okay, it looks like someone had lots of fun today," Josh chuckled. "Emma, did you have as much fun as your sister?"

"I had *so* much fun," Emma confirmed. "We hiked on a mountain, and rode a pony and petted alpacas and everything. I got to give the pony an apple too," the little girl's face was wreathed in smiles. "His lips tickled my hand."

"They were both very good, and the animals enjoyed them as much as they like the animals," Annie smiled. "We'll have to do that again sometime."

"You are absolutely awesome, Annie. Did I ever tell you that?" Olivia hugged her friend, who was like a second mother to her. "You and Abby took care of the kids all day, gave them a wonderfully fun day, and now you're cooking dinner? How did I get so lucky to have you in my life?"

"Oh pish," Annie dismissed that with a red faced grin. "Abby and I enjoyed every minute of it, and before you start about dinner, you should know it is nothing at all special . . . only roasted veggies and mashed potatoes with tomato soup."

"Only," Olivia scoffed, laughing. "Like I don't know exactly how much veggie chopping is required for that. Thanks for everything, Annie." She hugged her again. "It is much appreciated, and I am really tired tonight, so this was a very welcome surprise."

"You're very welcome; now you and that man of yours need to both get washed up for dinner," Annie smiled to soften the scolding tone.

Olivia and Josh obediently headed for the two downstairs bathrooms to do her bidding, as Emma sat in her chair at the table. Annie lifted Sophia into her high chair then started bringing the food to the table.

"I already fed Molly and Sheyna, since you were running so late," she informed Olivia as she reentered the kitchen. "They were looking a might forlorn, and I didn't want to make them wait."

"Thanks, Annie, that's perfect," Olivia smiled. "I never expected to be this late, but it started snowing earlier than I thought it would, and heavier too. It was like slick mashed potatoes down in the lower valley."

"Yeah, that's never fun to drive in," Annie agreed. "Glad you made it home safely."

Josh sat next to Olivia, after pulling out her chair and Annie's too as Annie finally sat down with them.

Dinner was a very lively affair, with the little girls still talking about 'pacas' and the pony ride, and Olivia giving Josh a brief rundown of what had happened at the courthouse.

He was as baffled as she was about the strange old man. Was he the murderer or did he just think Olivia was someone he knew? Maybe she looked like someone from his past or something.

Annie got up and started to clear the table when they were done, but Olivia and Josh stood firm and refused to allow her to touch the dishes.

"You have done so much for us already today," Josh was adamant. "You will go sit by the fire have some wine, brandy or coffee and relax, Annie."

Annie and Olivia both chuckled at his stern expression.

"I think he means it, Annie," Olivia said with a giggle. "Which drink would you prefer?"

"I think it had better be decaf coffee, actually, Livvie. I have to drive home."

Olivia walked to the window and peeked out. "Actually, I don't think you're going to be driving anywhere tonight, Annie. It's like a blizzard out there."

Annie joined her at the window. "Oh my, it's really coming down, isn't it?"

"You're going to have to spend the night, Annie; I'm sorry for the inconvenience." Olivia said contritely. "I'm sure you'd rather be home in peace after such an exhausting day."

"Not at all," Annie declared. "Livvie, you know me better than that. I love being around you and the girls, all four of them."

"I'll make up the guestroom for you. Would you prefer pajamas or a nightgown?"

"I'm fine with either one, thanks, Liv." Annie yawned, "I guess it's a good thing I'm staying over after all; I'm getting sleepy all of a sudden."

Emma came to say goodnight and hugged Annie sleepily. She followed Josh as he carried the sound asleep Sophia upstairs to put her in her crib.

Olivia quickly made the bed in the guestroom, then went up to tuck her daughters into bed.

She brought a nightgown down for Annie, who promptly excused herself for the night.

"Well, Josh, it's a good thing Julie is on the night shift still. I know she won't mind you sleeping in her room. I'll make the bed for you, but I don't have any pajamas that will fit you." Olivia chuckled.

"That's okay, Sweetheart," he hugged her. "I actually have everything I need in the car. You know I always keep my emergency bag there." He opened the front door, and the wind rushed in, bringing snow with it.

"Wow," Josh and Olivia both jumped back as he shut the door quickly.

"That really is a blizzard," Olivia gasped. "Maybe you should just sleep in your underwear."

"I think that might be a good idea," Josh agreed, looking at the snow that had blown in from the two seconds the door had been open. "It's fierce out there."

Josh wiped up the snow from the floor, while Olivia made up Julie's bed with clean sheets for him.

Josh headed to the bathroom to wash up before bed, while Olivia let Molly out back, opening and shutting the door quickly, and keeping watch through the window.

As she opened the door to let her back in, there was a huge crashing sound from the front of the house.

Olivia, Molly and Josh all came running from different parts of the house, almost colliding with each other as they reached the living room.

The wind was howling into the room through the broken living room window, and glass was shattered all over the floor. A paper wrapped brick lay in the center of the glass.

They heard the sound of a car driving quickly away through the snow, and could see the taillights fishtailing down the street before disappearing in the snow.

"Do you have any plywood, Livvie?" Josh asked quickly, as the snow and wind blew through the room, quickly chilling them to the bone.

"It's in the shed out back," Olivia said in a stunned voice. "I'll get it."

"No, you stay here and call 911," Josh voice was firm. "That wind is too strong." He hurried out the door, pushing Molly back inside as she tried to follow him.

Olivia quickly shut Molly and Sheyna in Julie's room so they wouldn't get cut on the glass, and ran to get a broom, dustpan and the vacuum.

Josh strode in carrying a sheet of plywood, and Olivia's electric drill and a handful of long screws he'd found in the shed.

"I'm going to get the plywood up, so the house isn't exposed to the weather, but, unfortunately you'll have to wait on cleaning up the glass until after the police come," Josh informed her, as he set the plywood against the wall."

"Yeah, I'm just really glad you can close off the broken window." Olivia smiled crookedly.

Josh took the broom to sweep the glass off the window sill, then got to work boarding up the broken window to shut out the snow and frigid wind.

As the last screw went into place, they both stopped and looked at each other for a few seconds, as the adrenaline subsided.

"I can't believe he would choose a night like this to attack." Josh shook his head at the amount of insanity needed to do that. "It's a full on blizzard out there. How could he even see to drive?"

"This is getting really weird, Josh," Olivia said worriedly. "He knows where I live."

"I had to let Dave off for the night. I couldn't make the poor guy sit out there in that, but I really wish I could have seen the car this guy was driving," Josh put his arms around Olivia. "Don't worry, Love, someone will be watching the house from now on, no matter what weather we have."

"Thanks, Josh. I'm sorry to get all wimpy on you. I just worry when it comes to my family's safety." Olivia grinned weakly.

A knock on the door, announced the arrival of the Birchwood police officers, who turned out to be Julie and Sergeant Lilly Meeks, their client, Elaine Williams's daughter.

It didn't take long for them to assess the situation, as the only real evidence besides broken glass was the paper wrapped brick. Julie took pictures of the room, and the boarded up window, then Sergeant Meeks asked her to retrieve the brick.

"Let's see what he has to say this time," she gestured toward the brick, in its by now, slightly soggy paper wrapper.

Julie pulled on a pair of gloves from her parka and carefully picked up and unwrapped the brick, opening the paper to read.

" *'Did you think I don't always know where you are? You're not safe in your house, much less in your car. You want to delve into the past, well this time just might be your last.'* "

"Okay, this has gone on long enough," Josh thundered, fighting the instinct to start throwing things himself. "I can't have you being in this much danger. This guy is a total nutcase."

"Shh, Josh. You're going to wake everyone," Olivia grabbed his arm, quieting him with a look and a soft touch. "The note is just his way of trying to intimidate us. We already knew he knows where I live once he threw the brick in my living room window." Olivia spoke in a quiet, but firm voice. "You can't let him get to you like that. If we stop investigating, he wins."

"I didn't say *I* was going to stop investigating, but I do think *you* should stop. Livvie, this guy is dangerous," Josh blew out an angry, exasperated breath. "He is stalking you."

"Yes, I can see that," Olivia said quietly. "I will be extremely careful, Josh. I don't want to get hurt, and I definitely don't want any of our girls to get hurt, but I can't just let him win."

Josh sighed, getting control of his temper, as Olivia's calm determination got through to him.

"All right, I can understand that, and I don't want him to win either. In fact, I really want to get this guy now." Josh gritted his teeth in annoyance. "If he was trying to get us to give up, he chose the wrong method."

Olivia hid the tiny smile that tried to sneak its way onto her face, as she realized how much very alike she and Josh were sometimes. Julie's face twitched as well, and she quickly looked away from Olivia so she wouldn't snicker.

"I agree," she said, keeping her face serious. "Intimidation techniques are not going to work with us . . . especially the silly Dr. Seuss-like poetry. We are professionals."

"Yes, we are," Josh stated, "However, I am putting people to guard this house twenty four hours a day from now until we get this lunatic. I don't suppose you'd agree to a bodyguard when you go out?" he added without much hope of a positive response.

"I really don't think that's necessary, Josh," Olivia replied seriously. "I will be very careful, and I won't go anywhere that seems at all dangerous. I totally agree with having a guard on the house until he is caught though.

"That is a great idea," Sergeant Meeks broke in with a wry smile. "I know Julie lives here, and that you're a former state trooper, but this house is off the main drag and fairly easy for someone to drive by and throw a brick or shoot a gun, but not as easy for us to keep a close eye on. We, unfortunately can't be here all the time, so if you can afford to hire someone, that would be an excellent solution."

"That's that, then," Josh nodded firmly. "I'll make sure someone is here at all times until this creep is behind bars."

"Okay, we'll add this note to the growing collection of poetry we have at the station then," Julie said, tongue in cheek. "You two should get some sleep. I doubt he'll be back tonight."

"I'm going to ask Abby to pass by Candlewick in the morning to make sure everything is okay. If this guy is following us, it might be better if we don't go there for now," Olivia commented as they closed the door behind the police officers. "I'd hate for him to start breaking the windows or doing something worse."

"That's a good idea," Josh nodded. "I doubt he is even aware of the house, as we haven't been there since he started throwing things at you, but it's good to make sure. It would be awful if he'd broken the windows and all the snow and stuff was coming into the house."

"I so hope not," Olivia sighed. "I guess we'll find out in the morning if Abby will check it out for us."

153

Josh and Olivia put on gloves and started sweeping the glass, Josh sweeping and Olivia holding the dustpan. They dumped the glass into the garbage can. Once they'd gotten all the big pieces, Josh vacuumed the rest to try to get the fine pieces, and Olivia quickly mopped the floor to make sure all the glass was gone, then freed Molly and Sheyna from the bedroom.

"We should try to get some sleep now," Josh hugged her. "Hopefully Julie is right and he won't be back tonight. I'll take Molly out back again."

"Thanks, Josh. Here's your coat," she handed it to him with a quick kiss.

He gave her a longer kiss when he and Molly came back in, with the wind almost slamming the door shut behind them.

"Sleep tight. Sweetheart," his face was cold against hers, the frozen snow on his hair and eyebrows dripping down his cheeks as it melted in the warm inside air.

Sheyna darted into Julie's room ahead of Josh, to claim one of the pillows, and Olivia chuckled tiredly as she climbed the stairs after Molly. Sleep would be wonderful.

CHAPTER THIRTEEN

Annie was astounded to hear that she'd slept through all the excitement of the previous night.

"I always knew I was a sound sleeper, but that's bordering on dead, I think," she shook her head, laughing at herself, as they ate breakfast.

Emma and Sophia were both interested in the broken, boarded up window, but Olivia and Josh decided to downplay it, merely saying that something blew through it during the storm, which was technically true.

"Well, one thing I've pretty well decided, I don't see how it could possibly have been Mr. Phillips or anyone else from the retirement center, driving around in that blizzard last night," Olivia said with a relieved smile. "After all he's been through, I would have hated for it to be him."

"That's true," Josh agreed. "You can ask Pam to be sure, but it's highly unlikely he could have been out last night with no one knowing, not to mention driving in that mess."

"That's something that's confusing to me, how many people would be capable of driving in that?" Olivia scrunched her face in perplexity. "I mean we are looking at an elderly person of at least seventy years of age, if it is the person who killed Jacobson, right? I'd have thought it would be hard for anyone to drive in that storm, but even harder for an older person to do it, since our reflexes are supposed to be slower when we get old, right?"

"Yes, they are," Annie answered, "Not only that, but there are other things that can make it harder for someone of that age to drive in such awful conditions. However, if he was very active, and kept his mind and body in good shape, it is quite possible for an elderly person to drive as successfully in a blizzard as someone my age or even your age, depending on how good a driver he was to begin with. I know people in their seventies who play tennis and you'd be surprised how well they play."

"Well, I guess I can't discount him completely then until I talk to Pam to see if he could have been out last night," Olivia sighed. "I am keeping my fingers crossed though, because I'd really feel horrible if he turned out to be the murderer."

The weather had improved enormously from the blizzard of the night before, but Josh groaned as he saw how much shoveling needed to be done.

"I think we got at least two feet and it seems even higher than that."

"I'll help shovel, Josh," Olivia grinned at his theatrics.

"You'll do nothing of the sort," Josh retorted chuckling. "I'm just feeling lazy this morning. I think it would be over your head anyway."

"Ooh," Olivia frowned in pretend anger. "That's a low blow." She tossed her napkin at him, as everyone laughed. "It's not even over Emma's head, is it Ems? Now Sophia, I'm not sure about."

"Can we play in the snow, Aunt Livvie?" Emma asked, hastily swallowing a mouthful of egg. "I wanna build a snowman."

"I don't see why not, Pumpkin, unless it really is over Sophia's head," Olivia smiled. "If it is that deep, we can shovel a nice patch for you to play and you can gather the snow you need for your snowman from the rest of it."

"Thanks, Aunt Livvie," Emma's brown eyes lit up like the sun. "I love building snowmen."

"Maybe we can go sledding too later if you girls want to," Josh added, drawing an even bigger smile from Emma's happy face.

Olivia chuckled as Emma bounced excitedly in her chair.

Sophia, looked up with a slight frown, as she tried to understand why Emma was so happy. She'd been busy eating her eggs and trying to pet Molly who was lying under her high chair and missed the whole conversation.

"We can play in the snow, Sophia," Emma told her sister patiently. "We're going to build a snowman and go sledding."

"No man," Sophia cried, "We pay no man." Her spoon flew through the air and landed on Molly's head.

Molly happily licked the egg from the floor, after initially jumping up in mild alarm. Sheyna looked on jealously as the egg disappeared under Molly's quick tongue.

"Yes, you will play snowman, Sophia," Josh laughed, picking up the spoon and wiping the egg from her mouth where she'd missed with a bite.

Olivia hopped up to get her another spoon and tossed the dirty one in the sink to deal with later.

Sophia took the spoon and used her hand to put another bite of egg on it, before aiming for her mouth. "Tank ou, Mama." She said around the mouthful.

"You're welcome, Sophia. You're doing a great job with your spoon, sweetie," she praised.

"Oh, Liv, I called the glass company and they should be here within the hour to replace the window,"

Josh informed her, as he rose from the table to help clear the dishes.

Emma got up to help, since Sophia only a couple of bites left, and had just gotten the last one in her mouth.

"Thanks, Josh," Olivia smiled at him, as she wiped Sophia's mouth and lifted her from the high chair. "It'll be nice to have the light coming back in. It's so dark in there with the board over the window."

Annie insisted on rinsing the dishes and putting them in the dishwasher, while Olivia cleaned Sophia up and changed her shirt, since she was wearing a fair amount of egg. She then quickly changed the bedding in Julie's room, so she could go to bed when she got home after working the night shift.

Julie arrived almost as soon as she was done, and headed straight to bed, looking like she was already half asleep.

"I'll be so glad when I'm back on the day shift. I feel like a vampire," she grumbled as she closed her door. "Have a fun day guys."

Josh put on his parka and gloves and went to work on the shoveling. Emma, happily followed him, taking one of the smaller snow shovels they'd bought for her and Sophia to use when they wanted to help.

The sun came out, and though the temperature was fairly cold, all the wind had died down. Emma had so much fun helping Josh, that he found himself enjoying the chore as well.

Once they had the sidewalk shoveled, the snowplow driver came and plowed the driveway for them, so they only had to tackle the small pile where the driveway joined the sidewalk that had been created by the plow. Josh did that alone, as the plow had compacted the snow, making it quite heavy.

Annie gathered her things and headed home, since Olivia and Josh planned to stay with the kids today. Molly followed Olivia and Sophia out of the house, while Sheyna decided to guard the warm, dry interior.

"Here comes the glass guy," Josh shouted from the edge of the yard. "Hopefully he can replace it quickly, so the house doesn't get too cold."

The man set to work, and after watching for a few minutes, the family went back to playing together.

"I'm going to go and make a little track for sledding in the back yard, from the woods down to the house, with my snowshoes," Josh volunteered.

"Thanks, Uncle Josh." Emma beamed. "Can I help?"

"Not with that, sweetie. The snow is too deep. Even with your snowshoes, I think you'd fall through," Josh grinned at her. "You're the most helpful little girl ever, Emma."

"I like to help," she agreed. "I like to sled too, so I will do that instead this time." She ran back to building the snowman.

Josh looked at Olivia. "She is so wise for her age, Liv. She amazes me sometimes."

"She really is. Have you been able to find out anything more on her mother?"

"Not yet," Josh sighed. "I put a call in to a friend of mine who may be able to help, but so far I haven't gotten any news from him. I know he'll get back to me as soon as he knows something though."

"I hope whatever he finds is good news for Emma, since I really do want what's best for her, but it's going to rip my heart out if we have to give her up." Olivia swallowed hard, and walked back to play with her daughters, forcing her face into a cheerful smile.

Josh walked through the gate into the backyard and donned his snowshoes which were hanging on a peg on the back porch wall, and proceeded to stomp through the snow relieving his frustrations about not being able to find Emma's mother, as he smoothed a nice trail down the hill for the kids to sled on.

He knew it would be as painful for him, as it would for Olivia, and probably for Emma, should they lose custody of her, and it was eating at him, not being able to get the information they needed. He decided to give his friend a call again to see if there'd been any progress at all.

"Josh,"

Olivia's voice brought him out of his thoughts, and he looked up to see all of 'his girls' standing in the back yard watching him snowshoe, except for Sheyna, who was sulking in the house due to the snow depth.

Olivia grinned at his surprised expression.

"It looks like you did an awesome job on the sledding track. Shall we give it a try?"

He shook his head to clear the cobwebs, "Sure, let me take off the snowshoes and grab the sled."

He trotted to the shed and quickly reappeared dragging the little smooth-bottomed wooden sled they used for sledding. He dropped his snowshoes on the deck and picked up Sophia.

The whole family climbed the little hill, walking in the packed snow beside the smooth track Josh had made. Josh sat in the sled at the top of the run and pushed himself off to make sure the sled ran properly and didn't run into the house or anything dangerous at the bottom.

The track was great, so soon the whole family was taking turns on the sled, with Sophia alternating between riding with Josh and with Olivia. Emma was proudly sledding by herself some of the time. Molly had great fun chasing the sled down the hill running, then sliding on her bottom half the time. She even rode in the sled with Emma a few times, though she jumped out the first time, turning them both over and causing Emma to slide all the way to the bottom on her belly, giggling the whole way down.

When they'd had enough of the cold, the little family trooped back inside to make lunch and warm up. Sheyna was given lots of pets and her feelings were mollified somewhat.

Josh made hot cocoa, which was a welcome addition to the grilled cheese, dill and tomato sandwiches Olivia fixed.

After the scary episode of the night before, Josh and Olivia felt themselves finally able to relax and let go of all the mysteries for the day.

Olivia whispered to Josh that she wanted it to be a perfect day for the kids, if possible, since the next couple of weeks would likely be super chaotic with her relatives and his dad arriving, and the wedding festivities.

They decided to make the whole day special, so after playing in the snow a bit more once their lunch was digested, they watched a Disney movie with the kids, took Molly and the slightly reluctant Sheyna for a walk down the road, and then after a light dinner, they roasted marshmallows in the fireplace for dessert.

Julie got up and showered, then joined them for the marshmallows before grabbing a bag of the sandwiches Olivia had made her, and heading back to work. It was obvious that she was not enjoying the night shift.

They were all exhausted from their active day in the outdoors, but in a good way. Josh headed home early, now that the roads were clear, and Olivia and the children went to bed soon thereafter.

CHAPTER FOURTEEN

It had been seven days since the night the brick had landed in Olivia's living room, and thankfully, there had no more scary incidents of brick or bat throwing or bad poetry since.

Wednesday morning saw Olivia and Annie rushing to get everyone fed, walked, dressed and ready so they could prepare the house for the arrival of Olivia's relatives.

Emma and Sophia were hindering as much as helping, but the adults knew they wanted to be a part of it, so they laughingly took it in stride, smoothing bedspreads and wiping tiny fingerprints from nightstands as they went.

Molly and Sheyna knew the drill, so they were careful not to assist by jumping on the newly made beds.

Olivia's assorted antiques that usually lived in the spare guest room had been moved to a storage room in Candlewick house a few months ago when Julie moved in, so with everyone sharing rooms, they would make do in the small house until the wedding.

Olivia had been gradually transferring most of their belongings to Candlewick, so the final moving process would be easier once the wedding was over and she, Josh and the girls all moved to the huge old mansion.

Josh had cleared his apartment thoroughly as well, leaving just enough to manage for the next week. His father would be staying with him, but his new dog would have to stay with Olivia, as Josh's apartment building was a 'no pets' building.

Julie was going to share her downstairs room with Emma, and Olivia and Sophia were upstairs in Emma's and Sophia's room, while Olivia's parents were getting her room. Her grandparents were going to be staying in the guest room downstairs, so they didn't have to climb up and down the stairs every day.

It was almost noon by the time the house was all set up and ready for the guests. Olivia was grateful that Annie had stayed to help, as it had taken longer than she thought to get everything rearranged.

"If you don't mind staying with Emma and Sophia for another hour, I'm going to run one more load of stuff over to Candlewick, so things are less cluttered," Olivia looked questioningly at Annie.

"Livvie, you know better than to even ask. I have never minded babysitting Molly and Sheyna, and it's even more fun for me now, with Emma and Sophia too." Annie shooed her away as she started making sandwiches for the kids. "Pack up whatever you want to take and get out of our hair," she grinned to soften her words.

"Thanks, Annie, as always, you are a lifesaver," Olivia hugged her and hurried to pack up a few more boxes and load them into her SUV.

The huge mansion was empty of contractors. Even Abby was absent. It was finally finished and ready for them to move in. Olivia blinked, realizing it was the first time she'd been alone in the house since they'd started work on it.

She unloaded the boxes and carried them into the house, one by one, carting the contents to their new homes as quickly as she could. It was almost time to meet Josh and head to the Portland, Maine airport, to pick up her folks by the time she was done. She washed her hands, and stacked the broken down cartons in the back of the SUV.

The house was so beautiful, and the grounds looked as lovely as she'd known they would, the first time she saw them, when it was a rundown, abandoned, spooky looking place. Now, it finally looked like a home once again.

She couldn't wait to see her daughters' faces when they saw it for the first time . . . especially Emma's. Sophia was too young for it to make much of an impression, but Emma was about the age Olivia remembered herself being when she dreamed of being a princess living in a beautiful castle. This house was pretty darn close.

Josh was waiting with the kids, when she pulled into her driveway. Annie had already left, and Josh had the children bundled up in their coats and mittens, and Molly and Sheyna were wearing their harnesses.

Olivia beamed at him, as she rushed up to give him a quick kiss and help get everyone into the SUVs. Since there was a limit to how many could fit safely in her car, Josh was following in his smaller SUV. They'd figure out who was riding with who when they got there.

They quickly unloaded the empty cartons and Josh carried them to the shed. Molly and Sheyna were fastened into their crates and Emma and Sophia into their car seats. And after making sure the front door was locked, they headed out, with Olivia leading the way.

The scenery was beautiful as always, driving through that part of rural Maine, and luckily the traffic was light, so they made good time, only having to stop once, for a potty break for Emma and to change Sophia's diaper at the same time, during the hour and a half drive.

The tiny waiting lot, where you were allowed to park for a while, as long as someone remained with the vehicle, had only a couple of other cars when they arrived.

They parked side by side and everyone got out. They walked Molly and Sheyna, in the small grassy area under the trees, then gathered to wait by the cars. Josh held Sophia and Olivia held Sheyna in one arm, and Molly's leash in her free hand. Emma was busy climbing up into the back of the SUV, and jumping down, over and over again.

It wasn't long before they saw the plane zooming down the runway, coasting to a stop somewhere behind the building. Emma hopped out of the back of the car and jumped up and down in her excitement. Sophia laughed and bounced in Josh's arms because her sister was excited.

Olivia laughed at their daughters, though Josh could see the tense anticipation in her face.

They had a few more minutes to wait, and Sophia decided she wanted down, so Josh managed to get her and Emma to sit in the back of the open SUV, and play with some of Sophia's toys to keep them amused.

Josh put his arm around Olivia and she leaned against him happily.

"I can't believe they're all finally here," she took a deep breath and blew it out. "I was so afraid Nana and Pop wouldn't be able to come, or something else would happen to mess it up."

"I knew you were worried, but I was pretty sure it would all work out just fine," Josh smiled. "I think you get a lot of your strength from your genes, so chances were good, they'd get here no matter what."

Olivia laughed, "You're right, Josh. I guess they are a lot stronger and more determined than I give them credit for being. They may have a couple of ailments, typical of older people, but they wouldn't miss my wedding for anything. I'm so glad Candlewick was ready so I could clear out the antiques and junk from the downstairs guestroom so they don't have to deal with the stairs . . ."

Olivia's voice trailed off, as she spotted the foursome exiting the door from the baggage claim.

Josh grinned as she jumped up and down like Emma had been doing earlier. They waved to her folks, and Josh took Sheyna from her and grabbed Molly's leash. He kept one eye on the kids, as Olivia raced to meet her relatives.

Olivia introduced Josh to her Mam and Da, Brigid and Patrick McKenna, and her Nana and Pop, Mona and Críostóir Duffy. After a lot of quick introductions and hugs, Olivia's parents, climbed into Josh's SUV, to ride with him, while everyone else rode with Olivia.

Looking at Brigid and Mona, Josh could easily picture Olivia at their ages. Both women still had a sweet, natural beauty, that despite, or perhaps because of, the lines creasing their faces, showed their love of life and their generous spirits.

Patrick and Críostóir were both fairly handsome men, Críostóir's face a bit more lined and weathered, than that of his son-in-law, but Josh could see traces of them in Olivia as well.

There was a lot of chatter, and Olivia and her grandparents shared all their news with each other during the ride. Emma was really excited to meet her great-grandparents, and Olivia had a knot in her throat, thinking how shattered Emma and everyone else would be if she had to leave their family someday.

If was pitch dark by the time they arrived at Olivia's house, and she escorted everyone inside, while Josh and her father brought their luggage.

Molly was as excited as Emma, and between the two of them, the adults were kept laughing while Olivia organized their luggage into their respective rooms.

Sophia had fallen asleep, and Olivia's grandmother sat holding her in the rocking chair, stroking her curly red hair and humming softly.

Olivia chuckled as she spotted Sheyna sitting on top of the highboy, watching in annoyed apprehension as all the people wandered about, getting settled.

Josh and his future in-laws got along immediately, and he knew right away, that his dad would like them too.

Olivia and Josh, fixed a quick supper of soup and sandwiches for everyone, while the visitors unpacked their bags and refreshed themselves from the long trip.

Olivia warmed up some leftover spaghetti for Sophia, as she was already too sleepy to be at her most cooperative, and sandwiches weren't really her thing yet, except for smooth peanut butter and jelly.

Olivia beamed so wide her face hurt, in her joy to have her family there, and dinner was a lively affair, even though everyone was tired. About halfway through, Sophia nodded off with her head on her plate, and everyone laughed as

Olivia scooped her up to go wash the spaghetti off her face and put her to bed.

Before long, Emma started nodding off a little too, so Olivia told her to say goodnight to everyone and get ready for bed. Julie had stayed to work a double shift, so Emma was going to have Julie's room all to herself tonight. As much as Olivia loved having Julie as a roommate, she was a little glad to have one less person there that first night. Everyone was so over the top that it was utter chaos.

Once dinner was over and they'd all sat around a few more minutes getting caught up on each other's lives, Olivia shooed her parents and grandparents to bed. They'd been travelling for over sixteen hours total, between the rides to and from the airports, so she knew they had to be exhausted.

"Whew," Olivia sighed happily, leaning into Josh's arms once they were finally alone. "That was so much fun and so wild I feel like my nerves are on overload," she laughed.

"It really was," Josh agreed, grinning. "Your folks are awesome. I know dad will get along well with them too." He rubbed her back, "It may be hectic, but it'll be fun and I have a feeling your Mam and Nana are going to take a lot of work off your hands in getting prepared for the wedding."

"I think so too," Olivia smiled. "They were already coming up with so many things they could do to help. Oh, Pam called and Mrs. Martin is coming to the wedding with her. Thank goodness I remembered to send her invitation."

"That's great, but, please tell me you're not going to be questioning her about the murder during the wedding,"

Josh joked. "You at least have to promise to say 'I do' before you go into detective mode."

"Aww, does that mean I can't question the priest?" Olivia teased, playing along. "I'd really hoped he could shed some light on the mystery."

Josh tickled her, and she squirmed away, laughing, then snuck up and tickled him back as he reached for his coffee cup.

Sheyna leaped out of the way as Josh gave chase, and Olivia jumped over the coffee table giggling so hard she almost missed and fell on the couch.

Molly barked and joined the chase, which put a quick end to their play, as they didn't want to wake the whole house with their shenanigans.

They collapsed, laughing onto the couch. Molly jumped up and flopped down across their laps demanding pets, and Sheyna joined them after watching to be sure they were done with their silliness.

"Livvie, I have some news I wanted to tell you," Josh turned serious. "I haven't had a chance to be alone with you all day until now."

Olivia's heart leapt to her throat and she swallowed hard. "You found Emma's parents," she felt the lump from her swallowed heart threaten to choke her. "We're going to lose her, aren't we?"

"No!" Josh smacked himself on the head. "I didn't start this right. It's good news, Liv . . . well, good and bad, I guess." He took a deep breath and started over.

"Yes, I found Emma's mother . . . or at least I found out about her. Her name was Ruth Paris. She was killed in action in Iraq almost a year ago, probably not long after Emma was kidnapped. One of the reasons it was so hard to find the information is that we were assuming she was a Private, when in fact, she'd been promoted to Corporal from Private First Class a few weeks before she was killed."

"Oh . . ." Olivia was stunned. "That's horrible. Did she know about the kidnapping?"

"I don't think so, no. From her military records, I was able to track down Stephanie Kelley, who was listed as Emma's caretaker for the times her mother was deployed." She still lives in New Salem, the same town that Emma lived in. Though she'd been staying in Emma's house with her while she looked after her, she is now back in her own apartment."

"Why didn't she report her missing when she was taken?" Olivia's voice was outraged.

"Because the kidnappers knew the situation and took advantage of it . . . Barry and Roberta Young also lived in New Salem. They forged a letter from Emma's mother, telling Stephanie that her sister was taking Emma and she didn't need her to be the caretaker anymore. Evidently, the forgery was good enough to fool Stephanie, so she let Emma go with her 'Aunt Roberta' and moved back into her apartment, never realizing that Roberta wasn't Ruth's sister." Josh paused to let that sink in.

"So her mother is dead . . . what about her father?" Kindhearted Olivia had tears in her eyes. "As much as I don't want to lose her, I didn't want her mother to be killed."

"I know you didn't sweetheart, and our wanting to keep Emma didn't cause it either," Josh kissed her tears away.

"Her father is listed as unknown on the birth certificate, and Ruth didn't have any other living relatives that Stephanie or the military knew about. Stephanie said her parents were dead. She was a little surprised when Roberta showed up, saying she was her sister, but as Ruth hadn't said anything about not having siblings, she figured she just hadn't mentioned her."

"So what happens now? How do we find out if she had any real siblings or any other relatives still living?"

"I'm taking a drive down there tomorrow, and maybe your Da and Pop would like to come with me, so you ladies can have the run of the house." Josh grinned. "The military records said Ruth and Emma were both born in New Salem, Massachusetts, which means it's quite possible Ruth lived there her whole life until she joined the military. Hopefully, in New Salem, we can find all about Ruth and Emma, and whether there are any other family members."

"Oh Josh, I am afraid to get my hopes up, but I can't help myself. I'm really sad to hear about her mother, but I so hope there isn't some other relative who will want to take her."

"Well, we'll cross that bridge when we get there, if we do. So far, it doesn't seem likely that there is anyone. She hired Stephanie, a friend of a friend, who had good references, to be Emma's caretaker, rather than asking a family member. The people I talked to at the army base, where she'd been stationed when she was stateside, said that no one had called or written to inquire about her." Josh spoke quietly.

"You'll call me as soon as you know anything?" Olivia's voice had a tiny catch. "I'm going to be holding my breath until I know."

Josh stood up, after gently dislodging the snoring Molly from his lap. "You don't even have to ask; of course I'll call you. I'm going to be holding my own breath," he smiled wryly.

Olivia slithered out from under Molly's hindquarters, and Molly opened one eye in an admonishment.

She walked Josh to the door and he kissed her goodnight before quietly slipping out to head home.

Olivia washed their coffee cups and checked on Emma who was sound asleep with her teddy bear in Julie's room Olivia bent to kiss her cheek and tuck the covers around her, before she went up to Sophia's room and crept silently in to kiss her too. She laid down on the folding cot in Sophia's room and stared at the moon shining in through the window for a long time before she finally fell asleep.

CHAPTER FIFTEEN

Olivia spent the day with her Mam, her Nana, her daughters and Molly and Sheyna. They drove into town to try on and pick up the altered flower girl dresses, the wedding dress and the matching bows for Molly and Sheyna. Luckily, the dresses all fit perfectly and all the little girls, including the furry ones wearing their bows, looked adorable.

Mam and Nana both had tears in their eyes as they watched Olivia and the girls trying on their wedding finery.

After they'd finally put the dresses in the car, Olivia drove them all to a little café that was pet friendly, for lunch. Once they were done, she suggested a nice drive in the mountains to see the still frozen landscape of snowy fields and forests, interspersed with icy lakes and waterfalls.

She knew her Nana would enjoy it, and was pretty sure it would be fun for her Mam and Emma too. Sophia was showing signs of an impending nap, so the drive would be a great time for her to catch her needed sleep, so she wouldn't be cranky later.

She chose the drive up to Crawford's Notch and beyond, so they could see the magnificent old Mount

Washington Hotel, as well as great views of the Presidential range of mountains in the background.

The weather was nice and it was a gorgeous drive. They stopped by the hotel for Olivia to take pictures of everyone with the grand hotel and mountains in the background.

When they were almost back to Birchwood, Josh called and Olivia answered, her nerves jumping as she waited to hear what he'd found.

Her Nana, who was sitting beside her in the front seat, wondered about the beatific smile that broke over her face, but didn't ask any questions when Olivia ended the call, seeming barely able to contain her happiness.

Olivia stopped in front of the house she and Josh were buying for their office, so they could see it, but since she hadn't brought the key, she couldn't take them in to really see it properly yet.

Josh, Patrick and Críostóir wouldn't be back in time to eat dinner with them tonight, so it would be a girls' night in, as Olivia jokingly dubbed it when she informed the others that the men would be arriving late. Julie, happily back on the day shift, arrived home in time to help with preparing dinner, and was brought up to date on everything they'd been doing.

It was a fun night, especially once the men arrived, shortly after dinner was over, with Josh's Father, Peter pulling in right behind them, bringing his new dog, Barney, a red merle Australian Shepherd.

It was a madhouse for a few moments, as introductions were made between the people and the animals as well. Soon, the people were all talking like old friends and Molly and Barney were running around the house playing while Sheyna looked on from a high vantage point.

Once things had settled down a bit, Josh and Olivia spoke together privately for a few minutes, then spoke with Emma in private, before the three of them stood as a group, in front of the others, with Olivia holding the sleeping Sophia.

"We have an announcement to make," Josh said in his deep bass voice that carried nicely over the conversation, silencing everyone quickly. He looked at Olivia, who in turn, looked at Emma and nodded.

"Aunt Livvie and Uncle Josh are going to adopt me and be my Mama and Daddy," the little girl announced with a huge smile and starry eyes. "And Sophia will be my real sister too, for always."

Julie and the older relatives all broke out in applause and congratulatory shouts, as they crowded around the little family, hugging them all in turn.

Sophia woke up and started crying, so Olivia excused herself while she took her upstairs and soothed her back to sleep, putting her into her crib and kissing her goodnight, before rejoining the happy circus downstairs.

Josh broke out a bottle of champagne that he'd bought along the way back from New Salem and they all shared a toast, Olivia gave Emma a glass of white grape juice so she could participate, since it was all about her.

Nana and Pop were the first to head to bed after Olivia had tucked Emma in for the night. Julie headed off shortly afterward, stating that she needed to be at work early in the morning. Mam and Da, didn't stay long after, and Peter retired to the den to read so Josh and Olivia could have the privacy they needed after a long day apart to talk about what had transpired.

"I called the lawyer and he is starting the adoption procedures for us," Josh hugged her, his eyes shining with happiness. "We already have the home study done and since we have been approved for Sophia, he thinks it will be smooth sailing with adopting Emma too."

"Oh Josh, I was so afraid to hope for this," Olivia smiled so hard her face ached. "I couldn't have stood losing her."

"Yeah, me neither," Josh's breath tickled against her forehead. "I think it would have been hardest on Emma, though. She's been through so many changes already. She feels safe with us and it's always been obvious that she wants to stay with us." He paused, "By the way, Emma's birthday is on the third of July. She'll be five years old, so she is actually only four still."

"I'm even more impressed with her verbal skills and her level of maturity then. Oh, Josh, I am so happy we can adopt her," Olivia leaned her head on his shoulder. "I've been terrified all week, and now all my dreams are coming true."

"Mine too, Liv. With all the crazy wedding planning we kept trying to do before we had Emma and Sophia in our lives, I think our wedding is going to be just as perfect as it could be, even though we had so little time to get it together after all." He grinned and kissed her. "I'd thought originally that I was lucky to get to spend my life with you and Molly and Sheyna, but now I'm getting to spend my life with you and four awesome girls."

Olivia smiled happily, as they walked to the den to let Peter know that Josh was ready to leave. "We're all lucky, I think ... and very blessed.

~~~

The next five days flew by like a blur, with no time for either of them to spend working on the murder case. There was so much to be checked on and then there was a bachelor party, which Josh had insisted be a very tame affair, and a bridal shower, with fun and sweet gifts from Olivia's friends.

On Tuesday morning, they had the wedding rehearsal, which was being done in a local park, in lieu of Candlewick, since they didn't want the children to see the house until the wedding, so it would be a surprise.

Abby and Olivia's Mam had used flagging tape in the park, to make a mock up of the part of the house they would be using for the wedding, so everyone would know where they were supposed to be.

It was fun and scary and awesome, practicing the wedding, and Olivia was feeling half jittery by the time they were done. She decided it would be a great time to run to the retirement center so her relatives could visit their old friends, and the girls could do their last visit before the wedding, the following day.

Josh, Mam, Nana, Da and Pop, all joined Olivia as she led Molly and carried Sheyna to do their visitations. Josh carried Sophia and Emma walked rather shyly beside them. Peter opted to stay at Olivia's house with the animals, since he didn't know any of the residents.

Pam's face split into a huge grin when she saw them coming.

"My, there are going to be some happy residents today," she laughed, hugging Mam and Da, then all the others. "It's so great to see you all."

"Why don't you join us when we visit the people on our list so you can catch up a little bit," Olivia asked her friend.

"I'd love to," she replied, ruffling Sophia's hair.

The group split, with Pam leading Mam, Da, Nana and Pop to visit their old friends while Olivia, Josh, the children and the animals went to do Olivia's weekly rounds.

The old people were happy to have the children as well as Olivia, Josh and the furry girls, and the retirement center was livelier than usual that day, with so many visitors.

They finally reached Mrs. Martin's room and once Olivia told her that her relatives were there, she asked if they could once again meet in the crafts room with Mr. Turner so they could all be there.

Once they had all gathered in the crafts room, the older folks had some catching up to do, and Josh and Olivia looked on, smiling happily as they realized Mr. Turner and Mrs. Martin were fast becoming very good friends.

The little group caught up as best they could in the small time they had, then talk finally turned to the murder investigation, and Mam, Nana and their men folk took Sophia and Emma over to the other side of the room to play with some puzzles they had sitting out for residents who enjoyed them, so the others could speak of murder without little ears listening in.

"We've both been racking our brains and discreetly asking around, but unfortunately we haven't come up with anything new," Mr. Turner said sadly. "I guess we may not be cut out to be detectives after all."

"Wait!" Mrs. Martin sat up straight, startling Sheyna, who had climbed into her lap. "Have you spoken with Nathan and Sarah Tompkins? Thomas Jacobson was Nathan's brother's lawyer, when Donald was convicted for running over that man from Vermont while driving drunk. He went to prison for ten years. I think he was sentenced to a lot longer than that, but he got out early for good behavior."

"No, I haven't heard anything about this before," Olivia admitted." Is he still living here in the valley?"

"No, he moved away when he got out, but I know there were a lot of hard feelings between his brother and Thomas Jacobson." She pursed her lips, "Nathan maintained that Jacobson promised them he'd get Donald off with no more than a year, but the judge gave him the maximum sentence since it wasn't the first time he'd been arrested for drunk driving."

"That's true," Mr. Turner interjected. "Nathan actually threatened to kill Jacobson, though I figured it was just anger talking and he'd get over it. No lawyer can ever be sure of what sentence a judge will give."

"Well, I can see why they'd have been upset if he promised one year and the sentence was for more than ten. Wow," Olivia blinked, "That's a large discrepancy. It seems odd that he'd make such a promise, doesn't it?"

"Come to think of it, it does," Mrs. Martin frowned in thought. "I can't remember who the judge was, but I wonder, now, looking back, if there wasn't some hanky-panky going on there and it didn't go the way Thomas had intended for some reason."

Olivia's face scrunched in thought, "I wonder if Jacobson could have been blackmailing the judge into giving light sentences." Her mouth dropped open, "That's got to be it. The judge, whoever it was, got tired of being blackmailed and didn't give out the sentence he was supposed to that time. Jacobson must have threatened him again and the judge killed him."

Josh was nodding his head in agreement, "I think you've hit the nail on the head. When we get home, I'll look up who the judge was on that case, as well as on the Phillips case."

"Mr. Turner, I have a feeling you and Mrs. Martin have just given us the information that will crack this case wide open." Olivia beamed at them and their faces showed their delight in being able to help solve the case.

"We'll see you both at the wedding tomorrow and let you know if the case is finally over." Josh grinned, getting to his feet and shaking hands with Mr. Turner.

After all the hugs and leave taking, the group left the retirement center together, stopping in the parking lot to decide who was to ride with whom.

Olivia asked Josh if he and the other men would mind taking the kids back to her house while she took her Mam and Nana to show them the house they were going to renovate for their offices. She wanted to get their input on how the layout should be so maybe they could be thinking about it while she and Josh were on their honeymoon.

The men laughingly said they were happy to avoid being involved in the talk of fabrics for decorating they were sure would ensue, and they decided that babysitting was highly preferable.

Olivia and her female relatives laughed as they climbed into Olivia's SUV, after securing Molly and Sheyna safely in their crates in the back.

Olivia parked and got the girls out of the back, carrying Sheyna in case she had any ideas of darting off somewhere.

She quickly unlocked the door with the key the realtor had given her, and escorted Mam, Nana and Molly inside, letting Sheyna down once the door was closed behind them.

"Okay, so we are planning to divide the house so that we'll have a nice sized office for the investigation business, another large area for my antique shop and then the rest for us to use as a daycare area for the kids, basically.

"We are thinking of using the whole upstairs as a living area for the kids and whoever is helping to watch them, while the family room will probably be our office and the rest, will be my antique shop," Olivia said, leading them around, showing them the rooms and how the house was laid out.

"That sounds like a great plan, Liv," Mam agreed. Let Nana and I go upstairs to see what needs to be done to make it comfortable for a living area, while you study what you need to do for the antique shop."

"Good idea," Olivia smiled. "I want Josh to be in on the office planning part of it but whatever we can figure out in the meantime will be helpful."

She turned toward the smaller rooms of the downstairs as the other women climbed the stairs, Nana holding onto Mam's arm on one side and the railing on the other side, as her knee needed a bit of help on the stairs.

I really do think the kitchen should be kept as a kitchen for us to use so we can fix our own lunches and even breakfast or dinners on the days we may have to be in early or late for some reason," Olivia perused the old fashioned but cute kitchen. *I feel like I just stepped back in time. It couldn't get much better than this for an antique shop. This house may have been lived in last during 1967, but I don't think most of the kitchen has been updated since the 1940s.*

She wandered into the next room, which looked like it had been a study or library, with a desk and tall bookcases. Walking over to the desk, she bent to look at an old dark stain on the hardwood floor behind the desk.

Oh my . . . is that blood? Olivia knelt to look closer.

"You know, it was in this very room that I confronted and killed that blackmailing scum." The old man's voice was cold.

Olivia stood up with a jerk, seeing the barrel of a revolver pointed at her face.

The man's pale blue eyes looked at her flatly. "It was only a matter of time before I had to kill him, once he'd started blackmailing me. I couldn't allow him to get away with that and I certainly wasn't going to let him ruin me."

"How did he start blackmailing you?" Olivia asked, trying to keep her voice from shaking. "Were you a criminal *before* you killed him too?" She tried with her peripheral vision to see if there was anything she could reach to use as a weapon, but nothing presented itself as likely.

"No, I simply had an affair with the wrong girl . . . one he introduced me to that was supposed to have been of legal age, but unfortunately for me, was shy of it by a year or two," the man's face twisted. "He had pictures of us together. It was all a setup so he could blackmail me into giving his clients either acquittals or light sentences."

"But you didn't keep doing it," Olivia stood still, praying her Mam and Nana stayed upstairs, so he wouldn't hurt them. "You gave Donald Tompkins a huge sentence."

"Yes, that's when I decided to show Jacobson that he couldn't blackmail me," the man sneered. "He thought I was going to give in and do what he wanted, but I was just playing with him, like a cat with a mouse. I gave him a couple of light sentences, then I slammed Tompkins with what he deserved."

"What did Jacobson do then?"

The old judge laughed, "The stupid mutt came and threatened to tell the world about my dalliance with that girl. He had no idea who he was threatening. I knocked on his door one night the following week and told him I was ready to do what he wanted, and that we needed to talk about his cases that were coming up."

Olivia heard a faint sound from behind the judge somewhere, "Did you talk about the cases?" she asked, to keep his attention focused on her, in case someone was sneaking around.

"Oh, we never got around to that, girlie," he cackled. "He led me into this room, seated himself at his desk and ordered me to take a seat across from him. Can you believe he had the audacity to try to order me around?"

"What did you do?"

"I pulled my gun and shot him. Unfortunately, I'm going to have to do the same thing to you, you know." His lips curled in a smile that only accentuated the coldness in his pale eyes. "It's a shame really, to shoot such a pretty little thing, but you didn't heed my warnings, so you've left me no choice."

"There's always a choice," Mam's strident voice broke the tension, as the huge cast iron skillet she threw broke the judge's wrist, sending his revolver flying across the room. The judge grabbed his wrist and howled in pain and anger, as Molly barreled into him, knocking him to the floor on his backside. Nana hurried to stand watch over him, brandishing another equally heavy antique frying pan, with a fierce look in her eyes.

Sheyna batted the gun away, as the now crazed man tried to lunge for it, then she chased it from the room, batting it with her paws as it skittered across the hardwood floor. Olivia, leaped from behind the desk and ran to get the gun before Sheyna managed to shoot someone, then she held it on the judge while Mam called 911 on Olivia's cell phone.

Josh arrived just ahead of the police with a huge screeching of brakes.

Olivia handed the gun to one of the officers, and Nana reluctantly lowered the frying pan, as the officers and Josh all stood with their mouths open at the scene in front of them.

Josh rushed to embrace Olivia, then as he assured himself that they were all okay, he started chuckling, picturing tiny, fierce Nana and the huge skillet. The police officers, grinned as they escorted the retired judge to one of their patrol cars, locking him into the back.

Two of the officers left with their prisoner while the others stayed to take statements from the women.

By the time Olivia had recounted the whole story of Mam's skillet tossing and Sheyna's gun soccer, not to mention the Molly bowling that had splatted the judge onto the floor, everyone in the room was laughing.

"Did you see Nana's face when she was holding that skillet?" Josh chuckled. "That guy was lucky you had a gun on him, Livvie. I think if he'd tried to move, Nana would have brained him."

"Right, and I would have too," Nana agreed in her thick Irish brogue. "Threatenin' me granddaughter like that."

Olivia hugged her and Mam both. "I was so afraid you would come down and walk into the situation without knowing he was there, and get shot." She laughed softly, "You were both awesome. You and Molly and Sheyna saved the day."

It was a celebratory bunch that greeted their guests that evening for the rehearsal supper.

Half the conversation was on the upcoming wedding, and the rest featured the capture of the murderous retired judge and the solving of a fifty-year-old murder.

The dinner was a fun and happy affair. Olivia regaled her friends with tales of her relatives' and Molly's and Sheyna's bravery until both Mam and Nana were blushing amid the cheers.

Peter, Patrick and Críostóir all stood as one and proposed a toast to Josh and Olivia.

It was obvious that the two families would be very happy being united by their children's marriage.

Mam, with her no nonsense way, finally called the party to an end, reminding everyone of how early they needed to be up and getting dressed for the wedding.

Once the other guests had gone, Josh and Olivia packed their families into the SUVs and headed to Olivia's house, where everyone piled out. Josh carried Sheyna to the door and set her inside, while Mam and Da helped Nana and Pop out of the car and into the house.

Peter carried Sophia, who was sound asleep, and took her upstairs to her crib, while Josh carried Emma, who had finally drifted off on the way home.

Once the children were tucked into bed, Josh and Olivia shared a sweet goodnight kiss.

"This is our last night as single people," Josh said in awe, as he looked into her eyes. "Tomorrow we will become one."

"I think it will be the happiest day of my life. I love you, Joshua Abrams."

"And I love you, Olivia McKenna," he kissed her sweetly, then stepped back as Peter joined them in the foyer.

"Goodnight, Olivia, my soon-to-be daughter," Peter chuckled, giving her a hug and a kiss on the forehead.

Olivia headed up the stairs with stars in her eyes.

CHAPTER SIXTEEN

The morning of the wedding was sunny and beautiful, with a mild temperature that caused Olivia to laugh in delight.

"It's going to be perfect for the wedding," she exclaimed to everyone at the breakfast table. "I'd hoped to get some pictures of the whole wedding party and the guests outdoors too, and I couldn't have hoped for a nicer day."

After breakfast, Mam and Nana helped Olivia and the little girls dress in their beautiful wedding finery, a few tears falling in the process. Mam's dress, brought from Ireland, as mother of the bride was of a darker green that complimented the bridesmaids and maid of honor dresses.

Molly and Sheyna had their pretty bows attached to their collars and the little girls had flowers pinned to their hair to match their dresses.

Josh and Peter would be helping young Jimmy Hill, who was to be the ring bearer, get dressed in his tuxedo. Jimmy's grandmother, Sally Tanner would be seated with their families, as Josh and Olivia both considered her a part of their family.

Olivia's eyes threatened to spill their own tears when she saw herself in Mam's wedding dress.

"Oh, Mam, it's so beautiful," she hugged her mother.

"No, my darling daughter, it is you who is the beauty, not the dress." Her mother wiped her eyes and then dabbed carefully at Olivia's eyes, as to not smear her makeup.

Mam and Nana had woven tiny white roses into Olivia's dark reddish brown hair, and let her hair curl softly, naturally to frame her face. She felt like the fairy princess she saw when she looked in the mirror.

All too soon, it was time to head to Candlewick for the wedding.

Da, who looked dashing in his tuxedo, drove, while Olivia sat in the front seat. The little girls sat in their car seats and Molly and Sheyna in their crates. Annie drove up to take Mam, Nana and Pop, since they couldn't all fit into the SUV.

Abby and Tiny were waiting to help them out of the car when they arrived.

Olivia hugged Tiny, Abby's boyfriend, and her friend, happy to see he'd made it back from the motorcycle convention he'd gone to. He looked awesome in his tuxedo.

Both sides of Candlewick Road were packed with cars, leaving enough room to drive by, but barely. The thoughtful guests had left the driveway free for the wedding party, and Olivia smiled to see Tiny's motorcycle with two helmets attached sitting in front of Josh's SUV. She loved the mental picture she had of Abby riding away on the back, her maid of honor dress blowing in the wind.

Emma was awed by the huge estate, her eyes wide as saucers, but Sophia took it all in stride, not paying any attention to the beautiful stained glass in the door's side lights. *She must think it is a church or something,* Olivia thought with an amused smile. *I wonder what Emma thinks.*

The women and little girls, along with Molly, Sheyna and the other female members of the wedding party gathered in the summer house to check makeup, sashes, bows and such, while the men were in the library of the main house, checking ties and cummerbunds.

Olivia felt like the butterflies in her stomach were playing bumper cars, she was in such a state of nervous excitement.

She brushed Sophia's curls back from her forehead and planted a kiss there, then did the same to Emma, who giggled sweetly.

"I love you, Mama," Emma said, so happy to be able to finally call her Mama.

"I love you too, Pumpkin," Olivia smiled. "You and your sister are so beautiful in your dresses. Do you remember what you are supposed to do?"

"Yes, I remember." Emma said proudly.

"I knew you would," Olivia hugged her, careful not to crinkle their dresses.

"Sophia, do you remember how to toss the flower petals like you did at the park?" Olivia asked the smaller girl.

"See?" Sophia scattered a handful of petals on the floor.

"That's perfect, Snookums," Olivia praised her.

Mam grinned as she collected the petals and put them back into Sophia's little basket.

There was a knock at the door of the summerhouse, sending Olivia's heart into her throat.

"It's time," her Da stood proudly, waiting to escort his daughter to the altar they'd made for the living room. "Nana, Pop, you should go take your seats so you don't miss anything. Brigid and I'll be bringing the bride along in a minute."

Everyone hurried to the house leaving Olivia and her parents alone.

"You look like a dream, Livvie," her Da's voice sounded choked. "I am so happy that you've found a good man like Josh. You're my little girl and I want nothing more than for you to be happy."

"Oh Da, I am . . . truly, ecstatically happy," Olivia hugged him, biting her lip to keep tears from forming. "And I am so glad you and Mam are here to walk me down the aisle."

"Shall we, then?" He held his arm out and she lay her left hand on his sleeve and her right on her Mother's as they led her to the house.

As she neared the open front door, Olivia saw Abby, Vicki, Pam, Julie and the little girls standing at the door. Emma was holding Molly's lead in one hand and Sheyna's in the other. Sophia was holding her flower basket happily, running her fingers through the petals.

As the bridal party turned to look at Olivia, the music changed to the Wedding March and Tiny, who was Josh's Groomsman, walked down the aisle, stopping to stand on the side of the room near the altar. He was followed by Andrew, who was the Best Man, then Peter and Josh. Peter took his seat on the left of the aisle after escorting Josh to the front. Josh stood next to Andrew, waiting for his bride to join him.

The priest followed, standing across from Josh, facing the aisle.

Next to walk the aisle, were the Bridesmaids, Vicki and Julie, and then Abby, the Maid of Honor.

Olivia almost got tears in her eyes again, as she watched seven-year-old Jimmy Hill, with the ring on a little white satin pillow, and Emma, leading Molly and Sheyna in their pretty sage green bows, and Sophia scattering rose petals from her little basket.

She took a deep breath and firmed her grip on her parents' arms, as they started their slow march down the aisle. Her parents placed her hand in Josh's, then lifted her veil and kissed her. Their eyes were damp as both parents took their seats in the front row of seats on the right of the aisle.

The little girls and Molly and Sheyna joined their grandparents in the front row on the right.

There were a lot of damp eyes in the house as Olivia and Josh said the vows they had each written for the other, then said 'I do' with a depth of love and certainty that was undeniable.

"I now pronounce you husband and wife," said the priest. "You may kiss the bride."

Josh lifted the veil, and even more happy tears were flowing in the audience as the couple kissed for the first time in their married life.

Josh and Olivia headed down the aisle, hand in hand, followed by all the participants in the wedding, including Molly, who was barking joyously at the excitement of the exit and Sheyna, who was being carried by Olivia's mother.

The whole crowd was laughing and celebrating as they threw rice over the happy couple.

It was such a nice day, that they all gathered outside for Olivia to throw the bouquet. She turned her back to the group of women who waited for it and threw it high into the air behind her.

It sailed way up before falling to land right in Abby's hands, much to Annie's delight. Olivia grinned as Tiny blushed bright red, with a big smile on his face.

They'd decided if the day was warm enough they'd have the reception half inside and half outside, so people could wander back and forth at will. There were a lot of people in both places and the atmosphere was as festive as it gets.

Olivia looked around her at the house and grounds and all her friends and family sharing it with them and knew their wedding had been even more perfect than she'd ever imagined it being.

The music started up again, this time playing a slow waltz, and Olivia and Josh took to the floor in the living room, sharing their first dance as husband and wife. Once the song had finished, Olivia danced with her father and Josh danced with her mother, while other couples wandered onto the dance floor to join them. Jimmy Hill danced with Emma, then with Sophia, and Olivia was glad to see that the photographer was capturing it all.

The caterers started serving refreshments and that was Josh's and Olivia's cue to depart for their honeymoon. They kissed the kids and Molly and Sheyna, then their other relatives and close friends, and slipped out the front door.

Olivia stood in amazement beside the beautiful rustic carriage, pulled by two dapple grey horses with flowing white manes and tails. She looked at Josh and her face broke into a huge smile as tears formed in her eyes.

"Oh, Josh, you are the most incredibly romantic man."

Josh lifted her into his arms and kissed her, then handed her into the carriage, stepping up to sit beside her.

As the driver flicked the reins, Olivia looked back to see the rest of her family waving to them, along with Mrs. Martin and Mr. Turner. She and Josh waved back until they turned at the bottom of the driveway and could no longer see the house, then he held her in his arms.

She knew she and Josh were embarking not only on their honeymoon, but on the first wonderful chapter of their lives together. As she leaned back against him, her heart was filled with joy.

RECIPES

Aracellys's Veggie Lasagna

1 Bunch Scallions chopped
1 Medium yellow onion Chopped
5 Cloves garlic Pressed
8 oz mushrooms chopped
10 oz shredded carrots
2 medium zucchinis chopped
16 oz Trader Joe's Multigrain Blend with Vegetables
15 oz ricotta cheese
16 oz cottage cheese small curd
½ lb Pecorino Romano
16 oz 6 Cheese Italian finely shredded
67 oz Prego Traditional spaghetti sauce
16 oz Lasagna noodles

Mix ricotta & cottage cheeses
Heat Trader Joe's Multigrain Blend to defrost (2 minutes in microwave)
Boil noodles until al dente
Sauté garlic until slightly browned, add onion, scallions, then later add mushrooms and zucchini
Cook until slightly softened adding salt, pepper, vegeta, oregano, basil, and whatever you like **not listed in ingredients

Pour a little spaghetti sauce in the bottom of the large ~~pyrex~~Pyrex and tilt to make it cover pan

Layer bottom with one layer of noodles, then a layer on veggies, then carrots, then Trader Joe's Multigrain Blend, then Pecorino Romano, them Ricotta/Cottage blend, then spaghetti sauce, and top with 6 cheese blend, then do another layer and as many layers as you can -fit. (Three is about it for the large Pyrex.)

Preheat oven to 375

Cover pan and bake for 40 minutes or until it starts boiling. Then uncover and bake until golden, approximately fifteen minutes.

~~~

Maria's Eggplant No Parm

3 oblong eggplants
2 cups Italian Bread Crumbs
Fresh ~~Parsely~~Parsley chopped (optional)
1 med onion, finely chopped
Olive Oil
Vegeta (a salty vegetable seasoning)
Black Pepper
1 - 28 oz can crushed tomatoes

Cut eggplants in half lengthwise, and criss-cross the insides, being careful not to cut through the skin. Each side should look sort of like a tic-tac-toe board, except with more lines running both ways.

Put bread crumbs and onion in flat bowl, add 2 ts vegeta, and stir in olive oil until moist. Takes a decent amount of oil.

Open eggplant with one hand and spread crumb mixture into cracks and cover top of each eggplant and firm down crumbs. (stuff them in there good!)

Drizzle a small amount of oil into bottom of ~~pyrex~~Pyrex.

Place eggplants into ~~pyrex~~Pyrex so they are flat.

Bake at 375 until crumbs are golden brown.

Remove from oven and lower heat to 350.

On stove top, in a sauce pan, combine 28 oz can of crushed tomatoes with 3/4 can of water. Add 4 ts of vegeta and black pepper to taste.

Bring to boil. Remove from heat and carefully spoon about 3 spoons of sauce over each eggplant until they are covered well, taking care to avoid disturbing crumbs. Spoon remaining sauce into bottom of ~~pyrex~~Pyrex.

Bake at 350 for approximately 35 minutes.

You can add parmesan cheese to this, but to me, (and I am a huge cheese lover) it really doesn't need it; it tastes like it has cheese already.

If you are interested in purchasing Vegeta and don't live in a place where it is available, here is the online vendor Olivia orders it from: Podravka Vegeta No MSG All Purpose Seasoning 500g

Made in the USA
Charleston, SC
11 March 2017